About *The Cutter*

"Virgil Suárez's novel *The Cutter* tells us more about day-to-day life in the first decades of Castro's Cuba than many academic texts . . . It captures the anger that compels one to risk everything and *tirarte al mar*—take to the seas on any craft that floats. The story of Julian Campos, his family, and friends is the story of so many people, both on and off the island, that it reads like a vivid oral history."

—María Cristina García, author of *Havana USA*

"A fine book."

—Vance Bourjaily, author of *Now Playing at Canterbury*

"In direct and uncluttered prose, Suárez's powerful novel . . . shows us how ordinary people can be driven to take extraordinary risks."

—*Publishers Weekly*

About **Virgil Suárez**

"Suárez is marvelous at creating believable characters."

—*New York Newsday*

"Suárez writes in a rough-and-ready style . . . He has an eye for detail and a gift for compression."

—*The Los Angeles Times Book Review*

"[A] gift for immediacy . . . Suárez's characters sound like my own family."

—*The [New York] Voice*

"The first young Cuban-American to enter the mainstream of American fiction. He plunges in with a distinctive voice."

—*The Palm Beach Post*

Also by
Virgil Suárez

Going Under
Havana Thursdays
Latin Jazz
Spared Angola
Welcome to the Oasis
You Come Singing

As Co-Editor

Iguana Dreams
Little Havana Blues
Paper Dance

THE CUTTER

Virgil Suárez

Arte Público Press
Houston, Texas
1998

This volume is made possible through grants from the National Endowment for the Arts (a federal agency), Andrew W. Mellon Foundation, the Lila Wallace-Reader's Digest Fund and the City of Houston through The Cultural Arts Council of Houston, Harris County.

Recovering the past, creating the future

Arte Público Press
University of Houston
Houston, Texas 77204-2090

Cover illustration by Matthew Archambault
Cover design by James F. Brisson

Suárez, Virgil, 1962—
    The cutter / by Virgil Suárez.
    p.   cm.
    ISBN 1-55885-249-2 (alk. paper)
    1. Cuba—Emigration and immigration—Fiction. 2. Sugarcane industry—Cuba—Fiction. 3. Sugar workers—Cuba—Fiction. 4. Young men—Cuba—Fiction. I. Title.
[PS3569.U18C88 1998]
813'.54—dc21   98-28337
                                                                CIP

This novel was originally published, in slightly different form, by Available Press-Ballantine Books in 1991.

8 9 0 1 2 3 4 5 6 7   10 9 8 7 6 5 4 3 2 1

To the memory of my grandmother,
AURELIA ISABEL GARCIA GONZALEZ
November 14, 1886–July 20, 1970
& for my parents

Las playas del destierro
no son tan bellas
hasta que se les dicen adios.

The shores of exile
are not as beautiful
until the final farewell.
—JOSÉ MARTÍ

THE NOTICE

1

Blackout.

Julian stares at the ceiling while the noise of a patrol helicopter drums into the room. Its vibrations shake the picture frames against the walls. Boom gone, the sound scales into an echo, a fading noise that reminds him of a flock of cowbirds fluttering up from a cane field, then turns into an overwhelming silence that creeps gently in the dark. Through the cone-shaped mosquito net, the darkness works strange configurations.

Who are they after?

The rain taps on the patio's tin roof, beats on the windowpanes, knocks on the banana leaves by the side of the house. He shuts his eyes and wishes he would, like a magician's rabbit, disappear and appear someplace else. Lightning flashes, followed by thunder, which cracks like rotted wood in the distance.

A mosquito caught inside the net buzzes, and when the buzzing stops, he knows that it has found his flesh, that it has smoothly inserted its stinger to suck a drop of his blood. He slaps his chest and gets the buzzing going again.

He can't remember having ever lived through such bad weather. The rain hasn't stopped since his arrival in Habana six months ago from the muddy cane fields of Oriente, where the army sent him to finish his last year of service.

As a child he loved to bathe outside under the rain, watch the branches of lightning fracture on the opaque clouds, listen to the sound of water running into gutters. But he has come far from his childhood, from those days when Bernarda, his grandmother, filled his head with tales of pirates and treasures out of books whose titles he can no longer recall. Certainly too far back to remember. A bird, he thinks, must have eaten all the bread crumbs he left behind.

So many things keep him awake. Anxiety invades him, straps him to the bed, and refuses to let go. Being rigid and too small, like an army cot, the bed forces him to sleep diagonally. He scratches an old mosquito bite on his sweaty legs, which lie on top of the bundled sheet. The itching starts . . . Eight o'clock seems ridiculously early to be in bed, but these daily blackouts last for hours, and limit moving about. Usually, by ten it doesn't matter whether the lights return, for he has surrendered to sleep.

But not tonight. Tonight the sounds of the rain and thunder and the flashes of lightning and the mosquitoes and the heat and the incessant croaking of the frogs won't let him. Heat and humidity make him feel as though he were back in the cane fields under a scorching sun, for his mattress is hot and the warm breeze that sneaks into the room keeps lapping his sweat dry.

It is as though he doesn't trust to close his eyes to the dark. To sleep. His thoughts come in bursts, like hand-grenade explosions. He takes comfort in the fantasy that everybody in Habana is in bed praying to all the saints and virgins for sleep so that in their dreams they may find themselves in a better place.

Julian tosses, turns, and searches for a cool spot on the bed, then, during a moment when a steady breeze makes the net billow, he feels himself float away into the freedom of sleep.

2

Bernarda's voice shatters his deep sleep as she calls from her bedroom. Confused, he pushes the net aside, feels over the floor for his shorts, and over the night table until he finds the *candelero* with the matches. *"Coño,"* he curses. He lights the wick, slips on his shorts, and rushes to his grandmother's room.

"What's the matter?" Julian says as he raises the fame over her bed. The flame turns the walls pale yellow. This close to her bed the air hangs musty with sickness and medicine.

"Door," she says in her tired voice. "Someone's knocking."

The knock comes again. His grandmother didn't imagine it, like the time she worried about a giant vulture perched on the roof of the house.

At the door, he pushes aside the window curtain.

"Julian Campos?" a voice says, then a light flashes across Julian's eyes.

"Yes?" A G-Dos, he thinks while unlocking and opening the door. Secret police.

The officer hands Julian an envelope, which he checks against the light. It is a telegram from the Ministry of the Interior.

"Expect another officer for inventory of the house," the officer says, while water drips from his raincoat onto the porch tiles.

"When?"

"I don't know, *compañero.*" The officer switches off his flashlight and walks away under the rain past the front gate, which he leaves wide open.

3

Julian closes and locks the door. After placing the light on top of the sofa's armrest, he tears open the envelope and reads the telegram:

PRESENT ALL DOCUMENTS IN ORDER
10:00 AM / MAY 3, 1969 /
ROOM 12 / THE MINISTRY
OF THE INTERIOR

May 3 is tomorrow. How like immigration to wait until the night before and deliver the exit notice in the rain during a blackout—that last little intimidation for people who want to leave.

"Who's there, Julian?" his grandmother asks.

Back in her room he places the *candelero* on top of her night table carefully so as not to knock over the two glasses, one in which she keeps her dentures.

"A G-Dos," he says.

"What did the bastard want?" she asks, sliding her hands out from under the sheet.

"He gave me this. The exit notice."

"Read it to me."

After he reads her the note, he inserts it back inside the envelope. He has been waiting for those words ever since his parents left the country. His grandmother even more so, worried it would arrive too late. "I might be six feet under by then," she had said.

She nods, then points a finger at the wall behind the headrest and says, "Please." Julian untangles her rosary from the crucifix he learned to make out of clothespins in grade school. The beads roll from his fingers into her cupped hand. When she tries to cross herself, she coughs. "You know where they are, the documents?"

"I know, I know," he says. "In the top drawer of your dresser. But aren't you happy we're finally allowed to leave?" Tomorrow morning, he figures, there'll be plenty of time to look over the documents.

"Damn government red tape. It took them long enough," she says, then coughs again.

"Water?" he asks, reaching for the glass.

He slips his arm under her neck and lifts her head from the pillow as her long bony fingers wrap around the glass. The asthmatic cough returns between swallows and then ceases.

"Better?"

"Wait until I tell Carmina."

"She's going to be happy. Carmina has been more than a neighbor and nurse."

"Go to bed. Tomorrow's going to be a long day."

"Can't sleep. I'm going to make coffee," he says, moving toward the door, which he secures with a wood stopper so that the wind won't shut it.

He takes the light to the kitchen, searches among cupboards for the coffee can, but finds it empty. He'll have to wait his turn at the bodega; and besides, he realizes, coffee at this hour will only keep him awake. His grandmother's right, he should rest. But he feels too tense, too excited to go to sleep, the same kind of excitement that made him want to get his life going when he got out of the service. Hoping he won't have to go to the Ministry of the Interior in the rain, he sits and tilts the chair against the wall, facing the living room.

In the room the old television set and cabinet radio take the forms of two fat men sitting opposite each other, engaged in a conversation.

The sound of the helicopter returns, this time stronger and louder, shaking the kitchen, rattling silverware and glasses. He runs his fingers through his hair as he stands to return to his room. The lights won't return tonight, he thinks, to hell with them. Overcoming his inertia, he bends over the *candelero* and thinks of leaving Habana. The note on the table disappears the instant he blows out the flame.

4

The crow of a rooster wakes him. He stretches, gets out of the net, rises, and draws open the curtain. A glare rushes into the room. When his eyes adjust, he sees that it is no longer raining. The raindrops that hang from the top of the braided wires fall when the chickens peck on the sides of the cage. He feels exuberant, overjoyed with last night's news.

In the bathroom he shaves with his father's razor blade while showering. Calabazar is more than thirty minutes from downtown Habana. It might be a good idea to take a taxi, since he knows how crowded buses get in the mornings. In his grandmother's room he tiptoes over to the dresser, pulls the top drawer open, and removes the bundled documents: their birth certificates, his service discharge, and passports. Before he leaves the room, he walks over to the bed and kisses his grandmother good-bye, for good luck. Her rosary is on the floor against the wall on the other side of the room. Wondering how it got there, he picks it up and puts it on top of the night table.

After making sure that the front door is locked, he walks away from the slippery porch. The thick smell of wet grass and mud fills the street. The kitchen light of the house across the street burns brightly behind the window shade. Julian imagines Fermin curled on the kitchen floor coming out of one of his hangovers. At the corner where the fallen leaves of Carmina's coffee plants clutter the sidewalk, he turns and heads toward the front of the bodega to catch a taxi.

5

Julian checks the bundled documents in his coat pocket one more time before the taxi stops, then he steps out, pays the driver, and walks up the flight of stairs that leads to the old Spanish facade of the Ministry of the Interior. From the ledge where an escutcheon of liberty hangs, the ash-colored pigeons coo and flap their wings. Julian enters through the rotating glass door and walks up to the information booth where a man in a blue uniform sits and stares at him as he goes by.

On the second floor, inside the room, two or three people work behind a Formica countertop: typing, filing, and shredding papers.

"Yes?" the man typing says. The click-clacking ceases. Julian takes the telegram out of his coat pocket and shows it to him.

"All the documents are here," he says, pushing them toward the man's hands.

The man reads slowly, his thin hands tremble. He puts the note down, walks to a filing cabinet, and, after opening the second drawer, he withdraws a manila file.

"When can my grandmother and I leave?" Julian says.

"Why isn't she here?" the man asks.

"She's restricted to bed by her doctor's order."

The man looks at Julian as though he isn't telling the truth. "It says here you were in the army, were you not?"

"Three years," he says, finding his dog-eared service discharge. "Long enough to lose my sense of humor." He smiles, but the stern look on the man's face doesn't change.

"In order for the exit to be granted, you'll have to do voluntary work," the man says.

"What type of work?"

"Cut cane."

"That's what I did last year."

"That was in the service, *compañero,*" the man says. "What are you doing now?"

"Attending the university."

"Wait here." The man walks away and disappears into another office.

So many concerns pass through Julian's mind while he fights fatigue—it will all be a mistake and he won't have to cut cane again, he assures himself. This time they'll let him go, for God knows he has waited long enough, played all their games by their rules! Five years ago they refused to let him leave with his parents, because at fifteen he had to enter into the Young Pioneers to prepare for the service. That day at the airport his parents were forced to choose: leave or stay, and they chose to leave.

6

Two airport security officers, guardias, *hold his father back. "Your son cannot leave!" the customs officer, a short, bald man wearing dark sunglasses, says.*

"Listen to me," his grandmother says to his mother. "Go! Elena, please go!" Then, as she and Julian walk to the window from where they could see the plane, she says to one of the officers, "Sons of bitches."

Julian's mother takes Ernesto, who shouts obscenities past the narrow corridor past the security checkpoint, by the arm and leads him down the boarding ramp. The guardias *take them out of sight.*

When the tow truck pulls the plane away from the terminal gate, Julian presses his forehead against the hard glass and waits for the plane to taxi to the beginning of the runway, turn, gather speed, the sun's glare flashing off its windows, and take off.

7

The man returns and informs Julian that voluntary work is inevitable if he wants to leave the country.

"But *compañero,*" he adds, "you don't have to go until we notify you. In the meantime, continue at the university. All right?"

No it's not *all right,* he wants to shout, he's so tired of waiting for notices, but instead says, "Listen, my grandmother's sick. I'm the only family she's got left. I can't return to the fields."

"I'm afraid that's impossible," the man says, closing the file and pushing the documents aside, "the preparations for the Ten-Million-Ton Sugarcane Program are under way, and . . . we need a lot of cutters."

"Program."

"A new goal to produce ten million tons by the end of the year."

"How long will I have to work?" Julian says.

"Depends. Four to six months. You'll be notified, *compañero.*" He throws the notice into the wastebasket.

Julian sees the man smile. If they only knew how much he detests that word. *Compañero* means for him a camaraderie he's never felt, not even when he was in the army.

"What about inventory?" Julian says. Inventory, being the final step in the exit process, would give him the security and assurance that he needs to believe that they are going to let him go.

"That comes after you've completed your work period," the man says, and returns all the documents.

"Bastard, *hijo de la gran puta,*" Julian says under his breath. He walks out toward the stairs. When will his waiting stop, when? Things would be so much better if they let him go—one mouth fewer to feed and clothe. Two. Outside, blocking the view of the ocean, buses crowd the streets and blacken the air with their exhaust.

8

Midmorning tranquillity fills the streets of Habana, usually a city full of nervous clatter. To wear out his anger and frustrations, he walks from the Ministry of the Interior to El Capitolio. Where did last night's rain make the people go? he thinks when he arrives at a bus stop and waits for the bus.

A police jeep drives by, and its tires splash water onto the flooded sidewalk, making ripples reach Julian's shoes. The cafes along the sidewalk remain empty, except for an occasional customer who wanders in.

Large posters commemorating the 52ND ANNIVERSARY OF THE OCTOBER REVOLUTION, which picture Lenin, Engels, and Marx, have been crossed out with paint and are now peeling off the walls. Another commemorates the 7TH ANNIVERSARY OF THE BAY OF PIGS VICTORY. They hang everywhere, unsticking, covering old propaganda leaflets.

Someone somewhere has to be testing his patience. Why is it necessary to go through all the trouble of drafting him into the Young Pioneers, then into the service, and making him cut sugarcane? To tease him with promises? To change his mind and force him to accept their ways? He cares very little for politics when all he wants and desires is to be left alone, to be free to choose what he wants to do with his life. Why put up with the fastidiousness of routines?

There are books Bernarda has told him about but which he can't read because they do not exist. But then how about the *guajiro* who couldn't read or write before the revolution and who is happy to be able to go to the library and read *Granma*, even if it is the only newspaper published?

Sometimes he wishes he had been born after the revolution so that he wouldn't know of a better way to live. Now at twenty they allow him to attend the university, and for what? The country needs engineers, computer technicians, architects, and doctors. All professions for which he feels no particular interest. Not knowing what to do, he has turned morose, ill-humored, and outright pessimistic, all from incertitude. He wishes he could change things, but . . .

When the bus arrives, he moves out from underneath the ledge and boards quickly. What will he tell his grandmother when he gets home? Two men sit in the middle, and an old lady behind the driver, who looks dizzy from the smell of exhaust. They all look up at him as he stumbles to the rear.

"You read about those two who got caught?" the man sitting near the window says.

"No, I didn't," the other answers.

"The fools tried to leave on a homemade launch."

The old lady glances nervously at the men, who laugh. "Got caught three miles offshore."

"*Granma* didn't say."

"The launch started to sink."

"Never learn, do they?"

9

Carmina stands facing the stove. From behind she looks like a Gypsy preparing lunch. She is a short, fat *mulata* with dimples on the back of her knees. The varicose veins. tributaries on her calves, look as if they might burst at any moment. Julian remembers that his mother also had them and that he poked at them when he was small enough to hang from her pleated skirt. "My circulation's bad," Carmina has told him.

"What's for lunch?" he asks, dropping the documents on top of the table.

Surprised, she turns. "How did it go?" she asks, wiping her hands on her apron. An unlit cigar butt hangs from the corner of her mouth.

"Back to the damn fields."

"But, Julian, that's absurd. Don't they have any mercy?"

"Those sons of bitches do as they please."

"Heartless degenerates. I thought this time there wouldn't be any problems." Steam hisses out of the mouth of the casserole. "Did they say what you should do?"

While Carmina finishes cooking lunch, Julian tells her about what the man at immigration told him.

"Your grandmother and I thought this time you were home to stay. No more military service or sugarcane cutting. Only the inventory and exit to look forward to," she says, then bites on the cigar, a characteristic he has learned to admire.

"Guess not."

The day Bernarda and he leave, Carmina, he imagines, will return to a life of seclusion within the boundaries of her house. She has been taking care of Bernarda since his parents left. She has no other family now except for Bernarda, whom she bathes and reads to before the afternoon siesta, and Julian, for whom, since his return from the fields, she cooks and does laundry.

He recalls his three years in the army while watching how quickly Carmina spoons some rice over his eggs without spilling any of it. He knows better than anyone, he thinks, the feeling of loneliness. It's like

15

listening to the sound of a frog from the garden, looking for it, but not being able to find it.

Julian asks her for advice although he knows there's not much she can say. Carmina tells him to be patient, that everything will work out to his advantage. "Remember how much trouble they gave your father. He was so desperate to leave that I thought he'd do something crazy. See, once they know that you want to leave, they do their best to make you regret it."

"Is my grandmother awake?"

"She's been sleeping since I got here."

As he sits down to eat, he thinks of a way to break the news to his grandmother, who'll undoubtedly take it as a bad omen.

10

He walks down the narrow, red brick streets of Cienfuegos on his way to his father's bakery from school. He passes the old people who wear their heavy, old clothes, for it is a windy day in September. Up in the balconies, the whack of women beating dust out of their rugs that hang from the verandas mixes with the chatter of the street. The women, enveloped in a cloud of dust, cover their mouths with their mantillas. Whack! In the distance a peanut vendor shouts, "¡Maní! ¡Maní tostado!" Children scurry like dogs from doorway to doorway, playing hide-and-seek and hopscotch.

At the corner of the winding street, the smell of fresh-baked bread greets him. When he opens the door a bell rings, but no one comes out from the back, where a radio plays a song by Barbarito Diez. From the stairs he hears the murmur of voices; and he follows the sound to where the black ovens emit heat, then up the dark stairway that leads to the small apartment where he lives.

In the living room, he finds his grandmother. He asks her what is wrong and she tells him two guardias *came and told his father he must turn the bakery over to the government.*

"We have to move," she says.

"I don't want to move."

"To Habana."

"When?"

"What's your father to do now?"

"They took him?"

"To the station," she says, "to sign the papers."

"Will I have to go to school?"

"You do."

"I hate school."

"You'll make friends fast."

"Don't care about friends," he says.

"If we don't move, they'll arrest your father and put him in prison." His grandmother takes him to the kitchen where, on the dinner table, she keeps lit candles in front of a plaster cast miniature of

San Lazaro. She gives him a glass of lemonade and a handful of salted crackers, his favorite afternoon snack.

11

All the rabbits hide in their boxes. A black-and-white-spotted female crawls out of its box to nibble water from the tin can by the corner of the cage. After she drinks she picks up a mouthful of grass and takes it back inside the box to her young, who are all descendants of two rabbits Julian's father brought home. What excitement he felt the afternoon his father carefully pulled two rabbits out of a jute sack. "Don't drop them if they scratch you," said his father, who that day wore a piece of rope around the waist of his worn khakis to keep them up—this had happened after his release from jail.

Napoleon, as his father named the male rabbit, likes to sleep with his ears sticking out of his box. Today, though frightened by last night's rain and thunder, he remains holed deep in seclusion. Julian drops fresh grass in all the cages, then calls the rabbit out of his box. "How are you today, old man?"

Being so big and old, Napoleon comes out slowly, dragging his long fat body across the wire bottom of the cage to sniff and eat some of the grass. While he sits, his red ears perk up, his nose and whiskers move up and down quickly as he chews.

Julian covers all the cages with an old, wet bedsheet and walks over to feed the chickens, who receive him with a clamor of cackles and crows. He removes all the eggs from the nests, takes them to the kitchen, places them carefully in the sink, and begins to clean them while Carmina finishes making dinner.

"I don't understand why she doesn't want to eat," she says, pushing a strand of her ash-colored hair over her ear. "You don't suppose she's giving up, do you?"

"You told her the news?" Carmina, he knows. communicates with his grandmother without getting her upset or excited.

"She asked."

"What did she say?"

"She cursed."

"Now she won't eat?"

"Old age, Julian. The only way is if I force-feed her like I used to do with my son."

"Whatever it takes." He's familiar with his grandmother's stubbornness. "Let me help with that," he says, and tries to lift the casserole off the table.

"No, I'm almost done."

Carmina sets all the plates, silverware, and glasses on the table. "Leave that alone," she says, "and come eat your soup before it gets cold."

Julian wipes his hands on his pants, then sits down on his father's old chair at the head of the table. He savors the soup while a light drizzle falls outside.

12

"The food's tasteless," Bernarda says, "and that wicked woman won't let me have a pinch of salt. Not a pinch." Her head is propped on top of two pillows; her gray hair spills over their edges. Carmina has washed, powdered, and rouged Bernarda's face. No longer are the blue veins visible on her sunken temples. The room smells pleasantly of rose water.

"No salt. Still you need to eat. Get stronger," he says, and smiles, sitting on the wicker chair by her bed.

She assures him that she will. But how could he convince her that she needs to eat? By scaring her? By telling her that if she doesn't eat, she'll . . . perish? He sits on the edge of the chair and remembers the last time she got sick, her doctor diagnosed her, and in the privacy of his office he warned Carmina that her illness appeared more complicated than just lack of rest. Carmina immediately sent Julian a letter telling him what the doctor had said. He managed, after much pleading to get a signed leave pass from Sergeant Aguirre. "She has bronchitis, high blood pressure, and a kidney infection," the doctor had told her. This happened seven or eight months ago and he'd like to think that his grandmother's health has improved.

The papaya and banana leaves cast shadows on the porch column outside the window. The shadows form intricate patterns. It is a cool, windy day, hard to come by this time of year, but cloudy.

"I couldn't sleep last night," Bernada says, "I kept hearing noises outside."

"The wind makes those leaves knock against the windowpanes."

"Like voices whispering," his grandmother says, and her black eyes narrow as though she were hearing them now

"Carmina should cook rabbit this weekend," he says, looking up at the bookshelf on the other side of the bed on which Bernarda keeps a glass full of *centavos* to honor Santa Barbara and an unlit cigar for San Lazaro.

"I can't eat rabbit, not the way Carmina makes it anyway," she says, "with all those spices."

"Chicken then."

"I don't know how she can sit at the toilet and be comfortable after she—"

"I get the feeling they're going to notify me soon."

"Oh, let's not talk about that."

"They're starting a new sugarcane program."

"Inventions, inventions, they never stop inventing."

"Sometimes I wonder why I just don't give up."

"Don't be foolish. What can they offer you?"

"Join the party."

His grandmother laughs, then says, "You in the party, come on, son. You are not party material. You've got a heart ticking in you. They need cold-blooded, back-stabbing bastards."

At one time Bernarda had sympathized with the revolution—even while it was still young and being fought high in Sierra Maestra. Later her son, Ernesto, was arrested and imprisoned for one year for organizing antirevolutionary activities. A false charge that almost cost Julian's father his life.

"There were times when I thought I could get used to whatever they put me through, and I did, didn't I? The service, the cane cutting, and I'll get over this."

"*Bueno,* that's the attitude," she says.

"They don't bargain fairly."

"They don't bargain at all. All we can do's wait, and you must eat, Grandmother, and get stronger, right? You are going to cooperate, aren't you?" he asks.

"Listen to you," she says, "don't you know a ship with holes on its hull can't float?"

"Eat and we'll find out."

This makes his grandmother smile, something he knows she doesn't like to do when she's not wearing her dentures. They have been irritating her gums.

As he leaves the bedroom she tells him to have faith, that she prays to God and La Caridad del Cobre for everything to get better and that he returns soon. From the hall, he hears her whispered prayers asking the Almighty to give her strength to be able to see her Ernesto one last time.

13

Blancarosa Calderon, the girl whom Julian has wanted to meet since he started at the university, sits next to him in history class. He knows her name because he has seen her write it. Her delicately penciled eyebrows stand out on her faintly powdered face. No matter how she looks, she always retains a sophisticated expression on her face. He likes the way she keeps pushing her rust-blondish hair behind her ear. And the vivid green of her eyes keeps him interested.

She hasn't said a word to him. On a few occasions, when their arms touch, he catches her looking at him from the corner of her eye, as if his sitting next to her makes her nervous. Something about her quick glances gives him the impression that she is trying to warn him.

At eight o'clock the professor, Señor Olivo, a bearded man with sleepy eyes, whose lips hide under a thick growth of hair, walks into the classroom. He sits down, pulls his notes out of his worn satchel, and begins the lecture exactly where he had left off on the last meeting: Siboney Indians. "Extinct," he says. "Imperialism's fault."

If the Siboneys saw their land now, Julian thinks, they'd gather their belongings into their canoes and paddle away to die in the treacherous currents of the Gulf of Mexico.

During the course of his lecture, Olivo frequently digs inside his shirt pocket and fishes out a foot-long cigar, then bites the tip off, spits it out, and lights the cigar, sucking until a cloud of smoke buries his face. His bad, gray-filmed eye always seems to be focused on Julian.

Blancarosa ignores Julian. For entertainment, he resorts to the large maps hanging from the side walls. The wrinkled and chalk-smudged maps show the hook-shaped island in the center of the blue Caribbean; none shows the tip of Florida. *El cocodrilo,* he thinks.

Julian tears a page from his notebook and writes Blancarosa: *What do you know about the Siboneys?*

BLANCAROSA
What do you want to know? Listen, you're going
to get me into trouble.

JULIAN
Who was their leader?

BLANCAROSA
If you paid attention, you'd find out. Hatuey.

JULIAN
Why don't you let me buy you a cup of coffee at
Las Orlas café after class? They sell great fritas.
We can study together.

BLANCAROSA
No. I don't know you, besides, I don't have the time.
Stop this right now. I don't want Olivo to point me out!

JULIAN
Olivo can choke on his cigar for all—

"*Compañero,*" Olivo says to Julian from his desk. "Open your
notebook. You'll need this information for the next examination."

Blancarosa sits still; her face flushes as though she's been insulted.
When Olivo resumes his lecture, she continues with her note taking.

Instead of taking notes, Julian draws figures, like the ones his
father taught him to draw. He draws a man holding a woman's hand,
and over them the devilish face of an old man. Over the drawing he jots
in large, bold letters, MAYBE SOME OTHER TIME! Then he pushes
the sheet of paper against Blancarosa's elbow, but she hesitates to look.

14

Days later he stands waiting his turn in the line that encircles the bodega. The afternoon rain has once again washed the streets clean. To one side of the building the bald *palmeras* grow tall in an uneven row. Giants. Behind them bulldozers dig and push, push and dig, flattening the ground with their steel claws.

The bodega used to be a train station. Long pieces of rail, now covered with weeds, lie strewn behind the building. Ties spiked into the ground linked by long pieces of rusty chain make the fence.

Printed on posters and glued to the side walls of the building, the word is out: SUPPORT THE TEN-MILLION-TON PROGRAM!

The line to get the food rations moves slowly. While in the service Julian learned to be patient, but lately time hasn't been moving as fast as he wants it to. He wishes he could be through with his voluntary work. This must be precisely what he hates most about his life, the waiting. Either he lives in the past, recollecting memories, or in the future, awaiting surprises. Notices. But never in the present, the now he wants to be free to enjoy.

"I wonder what it is that they are really going to build there?" one of the people in front of Julian says. He watches the balding head move.

"Maybe it'll be another base."

"In the city? I've heard rumors it might be Lenin Park." Julian leans against the side of the bodega and slides his hands deep against the seam of his pockets. The line up front curves and zigzags and turns at the corner. Heads move constantly. Some of the men have their ration books in their jute shirt pockets, while others use them as fans. Julian has tucked all three booklets in his back pocket.

"I'm so tired," the man behind Julian says to the woman next to him. "By the time we get our turn everything'll be gone."

The woman agrees. "They should make this go by alphabetical order, you know," she says. "Have a system to follow."

"That's a good idea."

"Have the A's, B's, C's, and D's come one day and then break up the rest for other days."

Her voice sounds distant, sad, as if she isn't used to frequent conversation.

"And the rations keep getting smaller," adds the man, making the gesture with his thin-fingered hands. "Three months ago everyone got two pounds of coffee, today we get one."

"What gets me angry's that the price of cigarettes went up again."

"I'm glad I don't smoke."

"*Mierda,* but I do."

How long will it take to get to the counter? Julian wonders. He hopes there'll be rice and black beans left. A young girl walks away from the bodega holding two bags, having, it seems, a terrible time carrying them. For an instant Julian thinks he recognizes her, then he is sure. The young girl is Fermin's daughter, Ofelia.

"I'm getting the hell out of here," a short black man with spongy white hair says. "I'm tired." The man's arms flap against the sides of his dirty coat. "Enough is enough!"

"There he goes again," the woman says.

"Papo's crazy, eh?"

"He's been wearing that same suit since I first saw him around here."

"He's quite a character, all right."

Away from the line three boys play marbles. The taller one wears a Young Pioneer school uniform with a silver star embroidered on his red beret, while the other two wear plain clothes. "Let's play for keeps," the tall boy keeps saying.

Julian arrives at the corner and turns to see that the line extends all the way to the long counter, behind which three men seem busy distributing the rations. The shelves behind the counter look empty. One of the men bends over one of the sacks and takes out three scoops of rice, puts them inside a brown paper bag, weighs it, and then hands it to another man. "Three pounds," he shouts. "Next!"

"Here, put everything in here," the woman wearing a scarf on her head says, giving one of the men a dirty pillowcase. Her ration is filled quickly and the man returns the case.

"Have your book stamped at the end of the counter," the man says, pointing to another man sitting on a stool. "One pack of cigarettes per person next time!" he announces.

Julian walks up to the counter and drops the three booklets on the scratched surface. He notices the numbers tattooed on the man's forearm.

We're out of black beans," the man says to him. "You want pinto instead?"

"Are you sure you—"

"Pinto?"

"Okay, pinto."

He sighs. The man bends over, puts a few scoops of beans into a bag, then throws the bag on top of the scale. The scale reads two and one half pounds. "I'm supposed to get four and a half," Julian says.

The man stops. He picks up the booklets and looks at them. "Why don't these people come get their own food?"

"Look, I've told you before, my grandmother's sick and my next-door neighbor takes care of her, so I do them both the favor."

The man takes two scoops more and pours them into the bag, making the scale read four pounds and a little over a half. He pinches out a couple of beans and makes the arrow behind the scratched glass quiver on the exact number. When the man finishes with the rations, Julian secures his arms around the bags, pays, and goes to the corner of the counter to have the booklets stamped. "Only one pack of ciga—"

"I don't smoke," Julian tells him, then moves.

Over the top of the paper bags, he sees Papo approach. Papo hurries by, says loudly, "This is all shit!" and leaves behind him the stench of soiled clothes.

15

"You've taken my seat," Julian says to Bernarda, entering the kitchen. She sits at the head of the table, her hair combed over her ears and held in a bun by two gold Spanish combs.

"She's trying to be the head of the family for today," Carmina says.

"Don't get used to it," he says, and smiles.

Carmina laughs, moves behind the chair, and puts her hands on Bernarda's shoulders. "Ever seen her looking this pretty?" Carmina asks.

"Wonderful," he says.

"Teasing's going to get the both of you nowhere," Bernarda says to Carmina with a pleased look on her face.

"Her family line has always had good looks, so she tells me," Carmina says to Julian, then winks. "Remember how handsome Ernesto was, or is."

"Judge for yourself," Bernarda says, and takes Julian's hand.

"Has she ever told you how she met your grandfather?" asks Carmina.

He smiles, for the story goes that Bernarda met Anibal, his late grandfather, because of a mean bull her father kept on the farm. One day the bull got angry, chased her father around the corral, cornered him by the gate, and almost stabbed him below the rib cage with one of its horns. Her father, who had a bad temper, roped and tied the bull to a fence post and with a club crushed its testicles to a bloody pulp. The old man called Anibal's father, the only veterinarian in town, to come and try to save the animal.

"If not the good looks," Bernarda says, smiling, "then definitely the temper."

"True, true," Carmina says.

They all laugh.

"The food smells delicious," he says to Carmina, who is still smiling as she finishes setting up the table.

"Bernarda doesn't want any," she says.

"Why not? Did you forget?"

"I can't. Really, son," his grandmother says. "I'll have something light later."

"These beans you got at the bodega are good, Julian," Carmina says. Then to Bernarda: "Would you have some if I strain them?"

His grandmother says no.

Carmina pours a ladleful over the steaming rice, cuts a slice of fricasseed rabbit, and puts it on Julian's plate. The aroma of the meat fills the kitchen. His mouth waters.

"Delicious!" he says, chewing.

"Good? You like it?"

"It's not going to work," Bernarda says.

"Don't be stubborn, Grandmother."

"The *café con leche* I had for lunch upset my stomach."

They eat in silence and are halfway through when Carmina speaks again. "I expect you to write to us every chance you get," she says.

"Write? They haven't notified me yet."

"Yes, Carmina, you sound as though you want him to leave."

"Heavens, no. But remember the two or three letters he sent from Oriente? That's only one letter a year."

"I told you," Julian says. "Sergeant Aguirre suspended the mail whenever not enough work got done."

"Andres wrote every chance he got," Carmina says absentmindedly, as if she were thinking about a particular letter her dead son had written to her once. Her light green eyes are remnants of the beauty she possessed when younger, but now they are part of a haggard face that is covered with wrinkles, moles, freckles, and hair over her upper lip.

Julian excuses himself and takes his leftover rice and beans outside to the chickens, which gather quickly and devour the rice in a matter of seconds.

"Quick, Julian!" shouts Carmina from the kitchen doorway.

He rushes there to find Carmina kneeling next to his grandmother.

"She fell," Carmina says, "and I'm afraid she's hurt her head."

"Grandmother!" he says, lifting her by her shoulders. Bernarda's face turns red as though she is choking.

"Leave her down," Carmina says. "She had a coughing fit."

Something has to be stuck in her throat, but she hasn't eaten. Air, she is gasping for air. "Grandmother!" he keeps shouting.

"She started to cough and lost her balance."

"Grandmother," he says.

"Quick, run to Fermin's house and ask Silvia to let you use the phone. Call an ambulance."

He runs out of the house, jumps over the front gate, and goes across the street. On Fermin's porch steps, he knocks hard on the door until Silvia, Fermin's wife, answers.

"Please, Silvia," he says, trying to catch his breath. "Let me use the phone. My grandmother's had an accident."

"Come in," Silvia says, opening the door. She points to the telephone. "But it might be better if you try to find a car to take her. A taxi. By the time an ambulance comes—"

Fermin walks out of the side room and slams the door behind him. "Where is it, woman?" he asks. "Where?"

"Fermin," she says. Her face grows pale.

Julian finishes dialing, feels every click on the line working on his nerves while he waits for a couple of seconds, but the line's busy. He decides to take Silvia's advice, runs outside, and waits by the side of the road until a vehicle approaches. When one draws near, he motions for it to stop. The car keeps coming, then, as Julian jumps in front of it, stops abruptly. Tires sliding over the loose gravel.

"Can you help me?" he says, walking around the front to the driver's window.

"Crazy!" the man says. "You belong in Mazorra." The man steps on the gas. Julian holds on to the handle, but it is too late. The car leaves him standing amid a cloud of dust. The instant another car drives up, he repeats the action.

"Where is she?" the driver asks, tossing his cigarette out of the window.

Julian points to the house.

The man turns and parks the car in front of the house. When the man gets out, leaving the engine running, Julian leads him to the kitchen.

"Carmina, let's go!"

Carmina dabs at Bernarda's forehead with a damp towel.

"I need you to come with me," he tells her. The man and Julian carefully lift Bernarda off the floor and carry her to the car.

Bernarda lies unconscious in the backseat. They climb inside the car and the man pulls away from the house fast. Her head rocks as the car dips into potholes on the road. Julian runs his fingers through her hair. Carmina, as if in a trance, begins to say over and over. "Chango, *kaguo kabiosile!*"

"What hospital?" the man asks.

"Calixto Garcia," Julian says.

"No, that's too far." the man says. "Las Hijas de Galicia's closer."

"There then," Julian says. He holds his grandmother close to his chest, close enough to keep whispering, "Not now, Grandmother. Not now."

The man takes out his white handkerchief and holds it out by the side mirror to let the traffic patrols know that he's going to an emergency. The piece of cloth snaps in his hand like a flag.

16

At Las Hijas de Galicia Hospital, there are no vacancies, but an ambulance takes Bernarda to Calixto Garcia in Habana. The hospital stands across the street from the university. In the waiting cubicle, Julian rests his head against the window which, high on the third floor, overlooks his classroom. Behind him, the wall clock ticks the minutes away while he waits for Carmina to come out of the emergency room. He hasn't been allowed inside because the doctor ordered the nurse to undress Bernarda so he could check her body for any possible fractures. The ticking of the clock seems to grow louder and louder.

People below on the sidewalk walk in a hurry in and out of the buildings, like ants. Students, he thinks. Everyone gives the impression that they have somewhere to go. Their lives, he contemplates, like his, have been given a pattern to follow, a structure, a routine: A student spends his time going from home to school, from school to the library or laboratories to prepare for the next examination, a soldier drills endlessly during the reenactment of a battle, and a factory worker labors for ten to twelve hours, goes home, chats with his family during dinner, sleeps, and before a blink of an eye, he finds he's back at work.

Footsteps approach and Carmina, as if burdened with the weight of her grief, enters the cubicle.

"She's coming to," she says, taking his hand and giving it a squeeze. Beads of sweat cover her forehead and the tip of her nose.

"What did the doctor say?"

"Nothing's broken. She's very weak, though. She has to stay hospitalized for a couple of weeks."

"Can I see her?" he asks.

"Don't make her talk."

His footsteps echo on the tile floor as he walks out of the cubicle and down the hall. He enters the emergency room softly, finds that his grandmother's body lies covered with a bed sheet that reads PROPERTY OF CALIXTO GARCIA HOSPITAL.

The nurses in the ward stare at him. He calls his grandmother.

The sheet rises and falls over her chest. He calls again. This time she responds by turning her gauze-covered forehead to him. "Son!" she speaks. "You've come . . . take . . ."

"Sssh! I'm here." He takes her hand, which feels limp and cold. "Rest, Grandmother. Rest."

The machine measuring her heartbeats begins to beep faster. A nurse approaches him. "She's excited now," the nurse says. "She needs to rest."

Tucking the sheet under her sides, he kisses her, then walks back to the cubicle. Carmina, whom he finds sitting on the carpeted floor with her legs crossed, asks him what she said.

"She mistook me for my father," he says, and moves to where he stood before in front of the dust-specked window.

"I spoke to one of the nurses and she said that later, after they're through examining Bernarda, they're going to move her into a room. She said I can stay with her for as long as I want."

He'll stay, he tells her, so that she doesn't have to make any more sacrifices. Carmina looks offended. "You don't have to—"

When Julian's mother had started to work as a teacher at José Martí Elementary, she paid Carmina to housekeep. Then later, after her husband passed away and Andres was drafted and Julian's parents left, she moved in because Bernarda, while watering the roses in the backyard, got tangled up with the hose, fell, and fractured her hip.

"Now listen, go home, rest, and bring me back clean clothes," she says. "You have school tomorrow."

The glare reflecting off one of Building 8's windows forms a halo of light. He thinks about Blancarosa. A sparrow flies across the yard and sits to sharpen its beak on the ledge of the roof.

"Julian?"

The sparrow flies out of sight. "Julian?" Carmina is saying.

"Huh . . . what?"

"What's wrong? You look pale."

"Nothing."

"Don't forget her slippers."

Lord, what are his parents doing for him? How could they have left him? If his grandmother dies, he might be refused the exit, for she might be the reason why they are still processing him. Slippers, bathrobe . . . He makes a mental note of all the things he is supposed to bring back.

Leaving Carmina alone with her prayers, he walks away down the hall, and as he passes by each room, the sick, worn-out faces of old men and women turn to him. Toothless faces. Faces on which there is no trace of faith or hope. Consumed bodies wrapped in hospital white. Pain, pain, pain. Walking down the hall in which all sorts of machines and oxygen tanks stand waiting to be used, he feels an electrifying chill run down his spine as he refuses to think that his grandmother might never leave the place. The sour smell of urine, vomit, and death abounds here, overwhelms. *Tap!* His steps sound. Tap, tap.

17

Later when he returns from taking the few extra things to Carmina and eats, he cleans the dishes and goes to bed. The house feels empty in the immense silence without his grandmother in her room. From his room he thinks he hears footsteps outside—the rabbits scratching their tin cans.

He knows he has had a nightmare because he awakes bathed in sweat and his mouth is dry. A rooster crows, perched on a broomstick over the empty nests.

Still half-asleep, he showers, shaves, dresses for class, drinks a glass of cold water in the kitchen and leaves.

Signs that read *GUSANO* greet him outside. *GUSANO* GET OUT! *Gusano,* worm, maggot, parasite of society. Paint has dripped from the paper and from the thick black letters that have been brushed on the wall on to the porch. *GUSANO.* A trail of paint extends from the porch to the grass, from there to the gate, and down the street in the direction of *El Comité,* the community watchdog. He follows the drops on his way to inform Nicanor, the person in charge, that his house has been vandalized, but no one answers his knock. Then, a noise comes from inside. The door opens and Nicanor appears shirtless and dressed in a pair of gray khakis. Lint sticks to his hair.

"Yes?" Nicanor says, then yawns.

"Come look!" Julian says, trying to remain calm. He complains to Nicanor, tells him all he needs to know.

Nicanor shakes his head and says, *"Compañero,* do you have any idea who might have done it?"

"If I did, I wouldn't be here now."

"Calm down. I'll have to write a report."

With a clipboard and pencil in hand, he closes the door, over which a COMMITTEE OF DEFENSE AND NATIONAL SECURITY sign hangs, and drags the cuffs of his khakis over the dirt toward the house.

"Do you know at what time this happened? Did you hear anything? See anyone?"

"I was asleep," Julian says, looking at the black letters. "Before I fell asleep, I did hear footsteps."

35

Nicanor scribbles something down. "Why didn't you get up to see who it was?"

"My animals make a similar noise."

Nicanor guarantees him that everything will be taken care of, then Julian asks him about the signs. "You can throw them away, but for the paint you'll have to wait."

Julian asks how long.

"Two to three months, depends. I'm not guaranteeing that the paint will be the same color."

By then he'll be cutting cane.

Nicanor asks him what happened to Bernarda, that he saw him and another man carry her into a car. Julian says as little to him as possible. After Nicanor walks away, Julian stands by the gate with his eyes shut, thinking that the signs are gone, that none of this has happened. Not to him. Maybe this has been his nightmare. *GUSANO.*

18

Familiar faces wait for the bus. Some sit under their umbrellas and others hold up the middle pages of *Granma,* while mist trickles over everything. The tangled skeleton of a kite dangles in the wind from the telephone cables. Two women sit and whisper on the bench next to a man in olive overalls.

The man in overalls frequently sits in the same spot, but when all the spaces on the bench have been taken, he paces up and down the bridge. "How much can a man take?" he says as he walks by Julian. He has POLAR BREWERY stitched in bright yellow letters on the back of his overalls. His father, Julian remembers, wore the same uniform during the days he worked at the brewery.

The crowded bus arrives late as usual. Pushing and shoving, the people gather at the entrance. Julian gets on last, letting the door hiss shut behind him.

Past José Martí Elementary School, which he attended, the empty church where he made his first Holy Communion stands a ruin. Chunks of plaster peel off the walls, while the bricks underneath take the appearance of chipped teeth, rows of red bricks with cement caked between them. Shortly after the stained-glass windows fell, the ribbed roof caved in.

On the round mirror over the sliding doors, he catches a glimpse of his tired face, his black sleepy eyes, pale cheeks, a thin bony nose, and colorless small lips, almost too small to be capable of smiles. And his straight short hair (growing out some since the last haircut in the service) seems unmanageable now that it has dried.

"Stop!" a voice shouts from the back of the bus. "I get off here."

Usually by the time Julian steps out, the bus is half-full. A great sea monster, he thinks of the bus, spitting out people, onward it swims down the ocean of tar.

19

Before Blancarosa comes into the classroom, he writes her a note asking if she wants to go to a pizzeria he knows of in Miramar. When she arrives wearing a red-and-white striped dress, he hides the note inside his notebook. Like a knot, her name forms at the back of his throat. "Blancarosa," he says, feeling a warm sensation rise from his chest to his head.

She turns to him. "Good morning, Julian," she says, and smiles.

He asks her how she knows his name.

"Who doesn't know your name by now?"

"Olivo bores me to death."

"He does, does he?"

Usually he's not a nervous person, only he hates to sit and listen, he wants to say, but instead says, "I'd rather look at you."

Olivo walks in at that moment, sits down, and begins to lecture. Throughout the hour, Julian watches the way Blancarosa writes down every word Olivo utters. He wonders how she might look in a bikini. The heels of her shoes look worn down to the nails that hold them.

At the end of the hour, he waits for her to walk out in front of him; that way he can come around and open the door for her.

"Thank you," she says, walking by him. Her padded shoulder brushes his chest.

"My pleasure." Perhaps they can go somewhere for a walk—El Malecón or Plaza Martí—or he can accompany her home. He holds the note ready in his sweaty hand.

The moment she walks out, an army lieutenant approaches and begins to talk to her. He puts his hand on the back of her neck. Julian watches them walk down the hallway, then turns away and tosses the crumpled note into the nearest trash bin.

20

Ofelia, Fermin's daughter, peeks out the kitchen window. He remembers what Bernarda had once said about her, that she would grow to be a beautiful woman; then she had been a girl with French curls that cascaded over her shoulders, who always wore colorful lace dresses. When he walks by, she points toward his house. He waves a hello, turning at the corner.

A jeep is parked in front of his house—finally he must leave to cut cane in the fields, he thinks. Two officers sit on the porch steps. Behind them, the sign *GUSANO* seems darker, taller. They both look up at Julian when he opens the gate and enters the yard.

"Julian Campos?" the one with the helmet tucked under his arm says.

"Time to leave, huh?" He climbs up on the porch to open the door.

"Accompany us," the younger officer says.

"Why? What happened?" He seeks an answer in the younger officer's eyes.

With serious looks on their faces, they remain silent.

Julian opens the door, throws his notebook on top of the sofa, and slams the door shut. He follows both broad-backed men to the vehicle. "What's wrong?"

He tells the officers about Bernarda being in the hospital.

Neither officer responds.

He climbs in and sits next to the officer whose helmet seems too small. The other one remains quiet in the back. He asks one last time.

"Formal charges'll be read to you at the station," the policeman in the back says. The motor cranks to a start.

Why are they arresting him? How will he get in touch with Carmina? Ofelia, he comforts himself, will tell Carmina if she calls, or when she returns from the hospital. But knowing Carmina, he thinks she might not leave his grandmother alone. He feels scared, lost in a labyrinth of unanswered questions, as if these two men are taking him away for good. To La Cabaña. El Morro. El Principe. They turn onto the main road. The butt of the driver's Soviet pistol protrudes out of the scuffed black leather holster.

The only police station in Calabazar is close to the bodega on the other side of the bridge. Once there, the officer driving parks the jeep, jumps out, removes his helmet carefully as though not to mess his hair, and leads the way inside. Julian feels his heart beat in his throat and his legs growing weak. When they enter the office, the younger officer escorts Julian inside a detention booth made out of oak and glass. Julian steps into it and sits on a steel bench. The other officer speaks to a lieutenant.

"Campos?" the lieutenant says, opening the door.

"I want to know why I'm being detained."

"Where have you been for the past few nights?"

"Home. Hospital. My grandmother—"

"Been out late?"

"Get to the goddamned point."

"You've been accused of posting propaganda."

"I've never . . . shit. Whoever made the accusation's got to be crazy," he says.

"We'll have to investigate the matter."

"I tell you, Lieutenant, it's a mistake. I haven't been around long enough."

"Six months out of the service is plenty of time to get involved," the lieutenant says, pronouncing *involved* slowly. "Anyway, you are detained until the investigation comes to an end and you are cleared."

"The son of a bitch who made the accusation made a terrible mistake."

"Keep your voice down."

"How long will the investigation take?"

"As long as necessary."

"My grandmother's in the hospital and I can't—"

"*Compañero,* I'm sure she'll be taken care of." Only when the lieutenant motions him to follow does Julian wonder what he can do to alleviate his condition. Entering a dark corridor, Julian finds the barred cells neatly lined from side to side. The lieutenant pulls the iron door of the first cell open, pushes Julian in, and shuts the door. He leaves without saying anything further. Julian sits down in a dark corner, where, after a couple of hours, he curls up on the cold cement.

21

Nights later he still hasn't been released. He has lost his notion of time, of what might be happening on the outside, but he has grown accustomed to the solitude. He hasn't eaten anything but his fingernails. The graffiti on the brick walls blurs.

As he scrubs the stubble on his face, the hard calluses on the palms of his hands scrape his skin. He wants to confess, and tallies the long list of sins, but to whom might he confess? To himself? God? Or to a committee organized by the party?

He imagines Sergeant Aguirre in full uniform seated at the head of such a committee, his cold eyes staring at Julian from under the visor of his cap. "A loser. That's what you are, Campos," he says, spitting out each word the way he used to whenever he got angry at his platoon. "No guts. You'd do anything for freedom, wouldn't you? Huh? You'd sell your own mother for it."

Julian's back aches from trying to sleep on the hard floor. He rolls over onto his side while he hears the soft rumble going on in his stomach. In one corner of the cell, ants crawl around the opening of the small hole. The sight brings back the smell of his own waste.

The cell blacks out.

In the dark, he listens to his heartbeats, counts them to sleep.

22

Sergeant Aguirre means to shape him into a man any way he can. There are the endless drills and the long marches. Long marches under the rain. Long marches in the mud. Long marches over sand hills, logs, and nets. Then the rigorous snaking under the stretched-out spools of barbed wire on which he tore his uniform so many times. The kick of his AK-47 knocks him down more times than he cares to keep count of through the make-believe battles enacted during July's hot morning. Tanks and heavy antiaircraft weaponry arrive with all their metal-creaking intimidation: then the loud shooting: then the parachutes mushrooming in the sky: then the explosions: then the rain falls and the ground turns to mud, and when he has to crawl over it it smears his uniform and boots: then the dark clouds of smoke from the firebombs and confusion.

23

The first thing that comes into focus when he opens his eyes is his dirty underwear and the green flies that swarm over it. The corridor door opens and the lieutenant enters. "Campos, get up!" he says, and taps on the iron bars with his shiny boot.

Julian gets up slowly, aching, pushing himself up with the support of the bars behind him. He listens to his bones cracking.

"A woman's waiting for you," the lieutenant says, opening the cell door.

Julian gives the lieutenant a harsh stare, but says nothing, then walks out to the incandescence of the lobby.

"What happened to you? What have they done to you?" Carmina says the moment he appears. She's been smoking a cigar, for the minute she approaches and embraces him, its odor turns his stomach.

"Nothing," he says, and looks at the lieutenant walk behind the counter. "Just a misunderstanding, right, Lieutenant?"

The lieutenant doesn't turn around to look.

She wraps her arm around his waist and helps him walk out. He inquires about his grandmother's condition. Carmina tells him that the doctor has said that she will be ready to go home soon, by the end of the week. "Did they say why they arrested you?" Carmina asks after he tells her what happened.

"They made it all up."

"When I returned to the house, Ofelia told me that they had come for you."

Carmina tells him to be strong. Strong. Daily she summons Chango and Yemaya to look after him and give him the strength he needs. He feels so weak and the pungent smell of cigar in her hair is so strong that he knows he will collapse the moment she releases him. They hold hands like an old couple as they walk to the bus bench. There he drops onto the bench next to Carmina, who gently places her arms around him and lets his head rest against her breast.

24

"Maybe it's not meant for me to leave with you," his grandmother says when he visits her at the hospital. "I don't know, Julian. I've struggled all my life for my family . . . "

She pauses, turns her face toward the side wall where her room window faces the ocean, and seems to fall under the spell of its blankness. Bernarda doesn't need to know, he thinks, about the arrest.

Julian stands by the bed close to the IV fork, his hands deep in his pockets among the loose change. "Get better, Grandmother. That's all there is to it. I mean it. You have to will yourself to get better."

As he pulls his hands out, the coins fall on the mattress and scatter next to her feet. "Are you listening to me?"

Bernarda looks at him. Her eyes possess a semblance of defeat, of all the years of suffering.

"Your father never imagined he'd have to leave without you. Your mother and I decided he had to get out for his own sake . . . He cares about you more than you think."

He disguises his dislike for this sort of conversation behind a nervous smile while an avalanche of emotions tumble in him. The way he has always figured it is his parents are there and he's here. Ninety miles of rough currents between them. He grips the footrest board, and his body tenses.

"What happened wasn't his fault," she says. "Your father is a good man . . . a good man . . ."

The door swings open and a young nurse enters the room. She smiles at Julian while he gathers the coins, and tells him that it is time for his grandmother's bath.

25

Nicanor comes a week later to inform Julian that he received his transfer permit notice from the Ministry of the Interior. Julian must leave for the fields immediately on Friday. That same morning after Nicanor leaves, as Julian gets dressed in his workclothes, drinks cold coffee, and searches through the kitchen cabinets for a sharp knife, he can't find the motivation to cut the rabbits' grass. He finds a knife with its mother-of-pearl handle chipped, puts it in a sack, and leaves.

A hot and humid day greets him when he crosses the street at the corner, away from the shade. He notices that the kitchen light in Fermin's house isn't on. Across the dump site, where ashes from burned trash encrust the ground, and past the tamarind trees, he leaves the houses behind.

The spot where he usually cuts grass rests on a slope that faces the only kiosk in the neighborhood. This hill is the only place he knows of where the grass grows in abundance, thick, and, unfortunately, it grows on government property. From here he watches a group of men by the kiosk. He drops the sack and knife, kneels, and begins to cut. The cutting sounds like old clothes being ripped. Little by little, the sack fills. He is tying a knot on the mouth of the sack when he hears the screams.

An officer struggles, dragging a man away from the kiosk. The man kicks and fights up a storm of dust, but the officer keeps a strong hold on him. Everyone watches the spectacle quietly, open-mouthed. "Let go, you filthy bastard!" the man shouts.

Papo is being removed. As soon as they disappear around the corner, Julian hurries down the hill and heads for home.

On the patio, most of the rabbits lie outside their boxes, some gnawing at the wire, while the baby bunnies stumble over each other. He removes the top of the cages and throws grass in. Napoleon sits still against the side of the cage. Julian reaches inside to touch him.

Stiff, Napoleon rolls over on his side.

Julian picks him up, holds him, notices the droplet of blood on his mouth, then drops him to the ground, shocked. Maggots crawl over the back of Julian's hands as he stands back. He shakes them off quickly. He thinks that perhaps someone has poisoned Napoleon—he'll have no more rabbits die. He will tell Carmina to sell the animals. Julian takes the empty sack, wraps Napoleon in it, digs a hole deep enough, and buries him under the papaya tree his father planted on the front porch.

After he finishes, he washes his hands thoroughly in the kitchen sink and then wipes them on the grease-splattered apron hanging from the hook behind the door. He shivers at the thought of the maggots wriggling all over his skin.

26

The afternoon before Julian's departure, Ofelia, who has sad hazel eyes, a tanned face, and light sandy hair, knocks on the door and tells him he's got a call from Carmina. He follows her back to her house, admiring how easily her hips sway. Carmina's hoarse voice sounds distant, tired. Saying good-bye to her seems always difficult. She assures him that she's going to do the best for his grandmother. As he leaves Fermin's house, Ofelia and he exchange glances, then she tells him to take care.

The night, as he walks to Nicanor's house, seems like a veil extended over the starless sky. Fireflies jump among the tall grass in the distance. Julian finds Nicanor talking to two other men. One of the men smokes, and the tip of his cigarette becomes a moving red dot. Another man leans against the wall, but his face is hidden under shadows.

"Excuse me," Julian says. Nicanor turns around.

"Hold on," he says. "The truck'll be here in a few minutes." He turns around, folds his arms over his stomach, and continues with his conversation.

Julian moves closer to the man leaning against the wall. "Going to the fields?"

The man remains quiet.

"Have the flashlight ready to signal the driver?" one of the other men suggests to Nicanor.

Nicanor reaches to his back pocket, and from under his open shirt, he brings forth the flashlight. He aims it at the ground and clicks it on. Insects quickly appear and fly under the beam.

Sitting on his heels now, Julian discreetly looks up at the man next to him. A truck turns at the corner. Nicanor signals.

"Let's go! Truck's here," Nicanor says when the truck stops. "Everybody in! Let's go!"

Julian climbs and sits close to the tailgate. The truck has its canvas cover pulled over the top ribs. Other men sit in the truck. He hears broken pieces of conversation between Nicanor and the driver, who mentions Perseverancia and the sugar mill there. The last man jumps in, the one whose face Julian hasn't been able to see. He doesn't recognize him, but finally when Nicanor comes to the back and flashes the light into the man's eyes, the face becomes visible: Fermin!

"Careful back here, eh," Nicanor says, raising the tailgate and locking it, then the truck moves down the street.

Fermin's expression conveys a feeling of dissatisfaction as they pass his house. Past the *GUSANO* sign and Carmina's coffee plants, Julian forgets Fermin. The truck veers around the corner then moves onto the main road. With the slow rocking, some of the men go to sleep quickly. They snore. Then others, heavy-lidded, follow slowly. Julian waits until everybody goes to sleep, then tilts his head back and closes his eyes.

The Fields

27

The barracks reminds Julian of the service. Motes float in the light that sneaks through the square windows. Close to the ground, on the corrugated-metal walls, rust has eaten away holes big enough for rats and cane snakes to come and go. The long rows of bunk beds, between which scattered leaves and cigarette butts lie strewn on the dirt, merge in twilight.

The driver assigns everyone bunks. Julian gets his toward the right side of the barracks, far from the window. He chooses the bottom bed so he won't have to do any climbing. Further down the center aisle, Fermin stands in front of his bunk.

"Eat a hearty breakfast tomorrow," the driver says. "You'll need it."

The acrid smell of too many men crowded into the barracks brings back Sergeant Aguirre's voice. Julian can almost hear it chasing itself around the corners. "All right, *maricones,* I'm going to mold each and every one of you into something useful!" Aguirre had told his platoon.

"The latrines are outside, behind the barracks," says the driver, "If you need paper, ask the barracks leader."

Julian smoothes the bedsheet, which is stained and has two or three cigarette burns. No pillow. While the driver tells them the trucks will take everyone to the fields after breakfast, Julian moves to the entrance and sees the water trough, which has gone green with moss and fungus, and next to it, the abandoned skeleton of an orange tractor resting on grease-stained wood blocks, and beyond, in the distance, the barbed-wire fence.

"Everyone's away in the fields," the driver continues. "Take this chance to rest. You're not going to get much of it here. Get acquainted. If you have any questions, ask your barracks leader. No walking about or visiting permitted. Lights are out by eight . . ."

From where he stands he can smell the dewy grass.

Tired from the ride, he walks back to his bunk, where he sits, removes his shoes. and stretches out on top of the hard mattress. Sleep is like a precipice, he thinks, down which he easily falls.

28

Voices awake him in the dark barracks. He rolls over and sits on the edge of his bed, then wonders if he has slept through dinner. Shadows and silhouettes fill the barracks; ghostlike they pass, and hide behind bunks. The thud of work boots add to the confusion, the nervousness, the rush to shower, eat, and sleep. Julian knuckles his eyes.

"What a day!" a voice says from the back.

"I'm beat. Goddamn!" another voice says. "Could skip dinner. I don't have the strength to lift a fork off a plate."

Julian feels a deep hollowness in his gut as he bends over and digs his shoes out from under the bed.

"Where's Pedro?" a dark figure says, entering the barracks.

"I guess he couldn't take being dirty for another day, huh?" someone else responds.

"He couldn't. I want my money," the tall, apelike silhouette blocking the doorway says. "Are the rest of you guys still in?"

Some of the men say yes, they are still in on the bet to find out who can go the longest without a bath.

A man comes out of nowhere from behind and climbs onto the top bed. "I see I finally get a partner," he says.

Julian remains quiet.

"Orlando."

Julian introduces himself.

"Get here this morning?"

"Yes."

"How many more came with you?"

"A truckload."

"All cutters, huh?" Orlando asks. He tilts his head back and exposes a ring of dirt under his chin. "They'll never get to ten million at any rate." He unbuttons his shirt and picks at his navel. What the short man lacks in height, he has in bulk. Julian has never seen thicker arms. The rolled-up sleeve on one arm reveals the tattoo of a large-breasted woman. "Nice, heh?" Orlando says. "The bitch stabbed me in the back. I caught her fucking a police officer. I plan to pay him a visit soon."

Another man walks by behind Orlando and gives him a shove. "Hey, *culo*, look where you're going! See this guy? Do your best to keep away from that bastard."

"Who is he?"

"Our friendly barracks leader. His favorite targets are newcomers like you."

"I'm not a newcomer. I have experience cutting."

"Have experience cutting cane."

Julian leaves Orlando, who sings *"¡Ay, Cachita, Cachita!"* and walks to the mess hall. With a tin tray in his hands, he looks over the crowded tables for a gap, a place to sit and eat. The steam from the mashed potatoes rises and tickles his chin as he zigzags around. He listens to the constant shrieks, laughter, and clearing of throats rising over the tinkling of forks scraping the last morsels from plates. Old hunger, they call how these men go about eating in the service. Old hunger.

"Move out of the way!" someone shouts behind him.

He steps out of the way, finds a place to sit in the center of a side table, and eats. A dozen dark, bloodshot eyes look upon his plate. The men slurp their water, stuff their mouths, and chew rapidly. The mashed potatoes and stewed vegetables taste like starch paste; they stick to Julian's palate.

"Hey," the man sitting in front of Julian says with a mouthful of potato. "Want your food or not?"

Julian shakes his head.

The man's unsteady, blistered hands grab the plate before Julian gives him permission, then pushes his cleaned-out plate aside. "You'll regret it tomorrow," he says.

Tomorrow's arrival can't be helped. He stands and hurries outside, where the silence of the night drowns the noise from the mess hall. The night feels serenely cool. He enters the barracks, finds his bed, and throws himself down on the mattress. Only sleep will save him from thinking. The sound of the men returning from the mess hall comes softly through the window.

Orlando returns and climbs on his bed. He tells Julian about how some of this land belonged to his father once, how his father hired cutters for the cutting season, but after the revolution the government took the land away and made it into a work camp.

"Who'd have thought," he says, "that one day I'd be a slave in my own place?"

Julian lies like a corpse and listens, listens. The mosquitoes and the noise keep him awake.

29

No sooner does the loud horn from outside stop than the commotion begins inside the barracks. The door swings open and sunlight breaks in. Julian watches everyone scurrying about getting dressed. A man skips on one leg while trying to loop the other through his pants legs.

"If you want to eat, better hurry up!" the barracks leader shouts. "The trucks leave in fifteen minutes. Fifteen minutes, people!"

Julian walks to the mess hall and stands by the stack of chipped trays. An overweight man in uniform leans against the wall by the door. His stripes are not visible from where Julian waits. At the end of the line, he receives his coffee in an aluminum can, then finds a place to sit all by himself and eats quickly, not being able to savor his eggs and slice of toast. He manages to remain alert even though his eyelids droop a little. When he finishes, he places the dirty tray on top of a cart and goes outside to the truck.

A driver in uniform stands by two pyramids of machetes and work boots. "Get one of each," he says.

Most of the machetes have broken handles, or nicked blades, so Julian grabs the best one of those left—he hopes it's sharp—holds it out in front of him as if to weigh it. There are no work gloves. It's good enough, he thinks, thin enough around the handle not to callous his hands. Choosing a pair of boots is different, for most are old and muddy, worn-out, with holes in the soles, and since the lace tips have lost their plastic wrap, they will be difficult to string through the loopholes and tie. The pair he picks out of the pile looks to be the right size.

He circles the stacks and climbs into the truck. All the men inside sit quietly, wrapping pieces of torn clothing around their hands, the way boxers do. They sit quietly, as if waiting for a judge to declare sentence for a crime they have committed. The other men stare at him from under the shade of their sombreros while he removes his shoes. After he slips on the other boot, he ties his shoes together and hangs them around his neck.

The truck moves.

Out of the opening of the back of the truck, the sugarcane fields grow and multiply in endless crisscrossed rows. The greenery creates a sharp contrast between the red earth and the pale, cloudless sky. The canes stand tall, thick at the joints on their stalks, some bushier than others, and some grow so tall that they bend against the rest. The fields turn black all of a sudden. The cane is burned to get rid of the prickles on the leaves so that they don't make the cutters itch. At night, he recalls, the fields around the camp where he was stationed burned. Some nights when he found it difficult to sleep, he looked out the window at the blazing fields, burning. Burning like giant torches.

30

Cutters scatter into the foliage. Perhaps they believe that the faster they cut, the faster the day will end—Julian knows this is false. Sugarcane is never-ending The cutters squeeze their way through, breaking, cutting, while he inches away from everyone. He likes to cut alone, which he goes about slowly. The steady sound of cutting takes him back to the hospital, to the city noises, to the patio of his house. A soldier with an automatic rifle strapped to his shoulders struggles over the cut cane, shouting to cut faster.

Nothing is visible in the distance except for the mill's smokestacks. The sun burns stronger in the sky, making the heat upon Julian's head unbearable. He looks down at the black stalks that cover the ground at his feet.

The man closest to Julian looks like Fermin for a second, but isn't. Fermin is taller, skinnier. What has become of him? Julian wonders while the man keeps cutting closer. Soon they meet. The man cuts in fast even strokes with steady hands, usually cutting through on first strike. He strangles the stalks with one hand and chops with the other. Strangle, cut. Julian's shoes bang against his chest and back as he stops for a moment and squints at the sky.

"What are you looking for?" asks the man. Then: "There's nothing there."

The man cuts away in another direction. His boots crush the cut stalks. Climbing into the afternoon, the harsh sun reflects off the sharp blade of his machete.

31

"Death's looking for the man with the longest hair." Orlando, whose face is so sunburned that the scar under his left eye looks more like a welt, sits cross-legged next to Julian during the lunch break. "But the long-haired bastard thinks he can outsmart Death. He tries everything to fool him. Changes his address, goes about the town hiding, sneaking, constantly looking behind him. Afraid. But Death, no matter how hard the man tries, still shadows him."

One of the drivers sits on the dented fender of his truck to listen.

"So the man shaves his head at a barbershop and then waits for it to come to him at a bar across the street from the barbershop. He plays pool for a while, then sits at the counter."

Some of the men in the uneven circle smile.

"After a couple of drinks, an old man, a very very ugly old man full of scars and open sores on his face, and with the stink of garlic on his breath, enters the bar and sits next to the bald-headed man. After he orders a shot of the house's best whiskey, the old man speaks to the bartender. 'I've lost him,' he says. 'Lost him just like that.' The old man snaps his fingers. 'Who did you lose?' the bartender asks, wiping the top of the counter with the tip of his dirty apron. 'Someone,' says the old man. 'Someone I wanted.' The old man swallows another shot and runs his black tongue over his bloodless lips. He looks at the bald man next to him. 'I guess,' the old man says to the bartender, 'since I can't let another day go to waste, I'll have to take this bald gentleman here next to me.'"

Everyone in the circle breaks into laughter. Julian joins in. The horn blows.

The men groan as they get up, and some, still smiling, pick up their machetes and slouch away from the road, kicking up dust. Orlando sings, "*¡Ay, Mama Inez! ¡Ay, Mama Inez! Todos los negros tomamos café.*"

The ache returns to Julian's back the instant he stands and returns to the area he has cleared. Under the charcoal, his black fingers look swollen, numb from being wrapped so tightly around the machete's handle.

Hours later, the sun descends behind the fields, squeezing its rays through the cane. The sound of strokes slows down and is replaced by the sighs of cutters.

The horn blows.

"Over," says someone, massaging his elbows.

"And all for what?"

The machetes and boots are collected and taken away.

"What are these fools afraid of? A machete is no match against a machine gun."

No one speaks as the cutters make their way over the cut cane on their way to the trucks. Once inside, as the trucks move out, Julian witnesses how his work slowly vanishes, slowly.

32

Julian asks Leandro, the barracks leader, where the showers are.
"I'll show you," Leandro says.

Julian follows quietly. Leandro has a broad back. His long hair, a dry, brittle mop, covers the nape of his neck.

Past the row of latrines, they walk around the building to a cemented square under a thatch roof. A man stands poised against a ladder, pouring water from a bucket into a drain canal.

"There they are," Leandro says with an encouraging motion of his hand, then he strips out of his workclothes.

Julian walks to the side of the paved square, removes his clothes, placing them on top of a fence post, and steps over onto the wet concrete.

"Three buckets each," the man pouring the water says. "Use them wisely."

Julian signals for the man to pour. The water runs down the canal and splashes over Julian's head. It feels cool and refreshing on his dirty skin. The second and third buckets follow unannounced. Julian sees Leandro at the other end looking in his direction.

"Your three are over," the man on top of the ladder says. "Get a towel!" the man says, digging with his hand into a large *canasta* hooked to the side of the ladder.

Julian walks over and grabs a towel. Then, collecting dirt on his wet feet, he returns to his clothes. Insects dart into the glass chimneys of the lanterns hanging from the guava-tree poles. The night is too hot to wear a shirt, even though the mosquitoes are bound to bite.

"Drop the towel in that other basket," the man says.

Julian places the towel there and heads back to the barracks. He feels too tired to eat, too worn out. As he walks past the latrines, he hears footsteps following him.

33

Cutting becomes bearable to Julian, who, during the past weeks, has adapted to the routines. Then one morning a loud voice wakes him up. He sits up on the bunk bed quickly. Leandro stands by his white bunk. Most of the men have gone to breakfast.

"I have something for you," Leandro says. "You can find out what it is for a price."

"I don't have any money," Julian says.

"You owe me, Campos. I'll pay you a visit come payday." He drops a yellow envelope on the dirt floor in front of Julian's feet.

The minute Julian sees it, he knows what it is: a telegram from the Ministry of the Interior telling him to return to Habana. "It arrived the same day you did," Leandro says.

Julian opens the envelope and reads that his grandmother has died.

"Bad news?" Leandro asks.

Julian looks up at the thin, pale face in front of him.

"My grandmother died."

"That's too bad."

"This telegram's three weeks late," Julian says. "I must go to Habana immediately."

"You can't."

"What do you mean?"

"I'd let you go, but I don't have the authority," he says, opening his arms.

"Who can I see?"

"There is no use in seeing anyone."

"No use, don't tell me that shit."

"The sergeant won't let anyone go under any circumstances."

"Where is he?"

"Believe me, you—"

"Where?" Julian's words sound as loud as thunder inside the barracks. He feels a rush of anger, and curling his hand into a fist, he prepares to strike. Some of the men peek into the barracks.

"Go to the last barracks."

Julian runs barefoot out the door. When he reaches the front door of the last barracks, he is out of breath, and his heart bangs against the walls of his chest. He knocks on the metal door. A shadow appears slanted on the corrugated wall. Julian turns to a man in uniform approaching to open the door. He is the same man who has been leaning against the wall in the mess hall.

"What can I do for you, *compañero?*" the man says.

"Look," he says, showing the sergeant the telegram. "I must return to Habana."

"I can't help you," the sergeant says, opening the door and walking in. "That arrived weeks ago."

"No one cared to give it to me," Julian says.

"I have strict orders not to let anyone go."

"Orders. What orders? This isn't a military camp."

"There's a lot of work to be done, and I have to make—"

"To hell with work, this is an emergency."

"So's the next fellow's and the next, *compañero.*"

"I'm not your *compañero,* you bastard!"

"Get back to work!"

Julian grabs hold of the sergeant's arm and pushes him against the wall. The sergeant's fat body makes a loud thump against the tin. The tin shakes as though the barracks is going to cave in. The sergeant struggles. Julian overpowers him.

"You are going to let me go."

"I don't have to do anything," the sergeant says. "You storm in here demanding—"

Two other men in uniform sneak up behind Julian and grab his arms, pulling him away from the sergeant. Holding him back.

"He'll come to his senses. You'll see," the sergeant says, fixing his shirt.

With all his strength, Julian frees himself and falls upon the sergeant again. The soldiers secure their grip, twisting Julian's arms behind his back, and hold him still in a stranglehold.

The sergeant pushes himself off the wall. Swings his fist into Julian's stomach. Immediately, Julian feels all the air go.

"Get him out of here!"

Obeying the order, the soldiers drag Julian out of the barracks in front of all the other men.

34

The soldiers lock him up in what looks like a storage room in the barracks, but it is now sectioned into smaller rooms and divided by barred walls. He can look out the window at the endless fields and breathe the fresh air. A bird occasionally flies by over the cane. Sitting in the corner with his bare back against the cold iron bars, he observes how blood oozes out and clots on the cuts on the soles of his feet he must have gotten from a piece of glass. The bleeding isn't important. He prefers hard labor to being kept from seeing his grandmother, but by now it is too late. She is dead and buried.

He feels his anger rising again, and he bites his bottom lip. He is angry because he wants to give up. How much more of this can he take? He tells himself he isn't a coward. His choices are limited, he realizes.

As the sun comes up over the barred window its rays light half the cell and force the other into penumbra. It becomes so hot that he crawls over the dirt floor into the shade. Yes, this same earth'll swallow his grandmother's body.

35

Later that afternoon he hears voices—all the noise of the returning cutters inside of his dark cell. He stands, pulls himself up from the bars, and looks out the window, but all he can see are the darkened hills to which thatch huts cling, slanted.

The door of the barracks unclamps open and a soldier pushes a man into the cell across the way. He leaves the man in the corner, dusts his hands off, and locks the door on his way out. The man faces the wall. He groans. "Bastard!"

Julian crawls to the front of the cell and sits leaning against the side wall. "Nice guy, eh?" he says.

The man's head turns in the dark, as though he is trying to recognize in which direction the sound is coming from.

"Across," Julian says.

"I can't see you," the man says.

"Your eyes will adjust."

"I got caught," the man says, "buying a bottle of *aguardiente.*"
Julian asks how.

"The guy who sold it to me turned around and snitched."

A likely thing to do, Julian thinks.

"He kept the bottle and my money."

"What's your name?"

"Fermin."

Julian can't believe it. He wants to laugh—who else would get caught trying to buy booze? "I know you. I live across your street. I sat in front of you when they brought us here, remember?"

"I remember. I thought you looked familiar." Fermin grows pensive for a moment, as if trying to recreate a vivid picture of Julian in his mind, to place him. Julian remembers the afternoon his grandmother fell and he needed to use the phone at Fermin's when Fermin and Silvia had argued.

"Why are you here?" Fermin asks.

"My grandmother died. I got into a fight with the sergeant. The *maricón* won't let me go."

"They are bastards. That's too bad . . . that she died."

"Did you know her?"

"I met her once when your parents first moved to our block."

"No use in going back now," Julian says.

"They've kept me sober long enough. I wasn't expecting this. Rotten food. Nothing to drink but murky water. What the hell's the army doing in charge of this place? I tell you, I'm dying to have a drink," Fermin says, and his voice carries the edge of his restlessness.

Julian tries to convince him that drinking's no way out.

"It is for me."

"There are other ways."

"What do you suggest? Should I revolt? Should I run to the streets and start a revolution? My own. We had a chance seven years ago. In October . . . but now. Machetes and stones and sticks are no match for machine guns."

Noises come in from the outside. Dinner is over and the men are returning to their barracks. A slight breeze blows in, steady enough to cool Julian's sticky skin.

"I wonder how long they plan to keep us here," Fermin says.

"Never can tell, but at least we don't have to cut cane."

Everything grows quiet. Julian imagines water squirting over his body—the man on top of the ladder pours bucket after bucket after bucket. Fermin falls asleep and snores. Crickets chirp louder from outside while the night turns darker. Something moves rapidly—a furry ball—along the edge of the wall and disappears around the corner.

Most of the lights in the thatch huts have been put out. Still feeling the pain in his stomach from the blow, Julian's mind rattles like a maraca.

36

Jagua Castle sits on top of a high cliff overlooking Cienfuegos Bay in which the docked fishing boats stretch and dry their nets. Julian stares at it from the balcony of his house. His grandmother reclines on an easy chair behind him and tells him about the treasures Cook's pirates hid in the castle long ago.

"Will you take me to see them?" he asks her.

"Maybe tomorrow. It's too late and the ghosts are taking care of it now."

"Were you alive when they built it?"

"No," she says, taking his hand. "I wasn't born yet. The Spaniards built it."

"Were they good, the Spaniards?"

"Sometimes. Sometimes they didn't understand other people."

"Who were the other people?"

"Indians."

He asks if the Indians were good people.

"They didn't bother anyone. They lived to hunt and raise their families."

"I want to see the ghosts," Julian says.

"If you look hard enough, you can see them from here."

Bernarda smoothes the wrinkles on her dress, gets up, and goes inside. Julian sits with his legs dangling between the wrought-iron bars of the veranda while he admires the castle. The darker it grows, the more he believes he can see ghosts floating in and out of the high towers.

37

Julian and Fermin pass the hours talking. In silence. Talking again. Agreeing things have changed. Some of the ways the country has changed Julian cannot imagine. According to Fermin, everything was better before the revolution. Julian believes him because he remembers the stories Bernarda told him. About days of abundance. Happy days. Days gone forever.

In the meantime, Julian fights back thoughts of his parents abandoning him. What happened happened, he contemplates, and there's nothing he could do.

"You know what I wish for?" Fermin asks.

Julian cannot begin to guess.

"I wish gasoline rained from the sky," Fermin says. He is excited and his voice cracks with a mixture of anger and frustration. Then he says, "Imagine two fireflies colliding in the night. Their spark and the gasoline would set this whole stinking earth on fire."

Imagine that.

38

"Will you go back to work peacefully?" Leandro says four days later.

Fermin awakes and rises behind Leandro. Dust covers his hair and clothes.

"You can't stay here. Look, *compañero*—"

Julian stands, walks over to the cell door, and grabs the bars.

"All you gotta do's cooperate. Go back to work peacefully."

"Do what he says," Fermin says.

"I can't forget that my grandmother's dead and buried."

"I don't want any trouble and I don't think you do either. You're here to do a job. You see, I know you're doing work because you desire to leave, right? The sergeant can make things difficult for you."

Julian nods.

"You are free to go if you guarantee not to create any more trouble; if not, you'll stay. The sergeant'll decide what to do with you."

"Tell him," Fermin says.

Leandro opens the door and steps over to the side. Julian walks out slowly.

Fermin says good-bye. Already there are men running about, talking, smoking before the trucks depart.

When he walks inside the barracks, he finds Orlando sitting on his bunk. He gets up when Julian approaches.

"Campos," he says. "Here." He throws Julian's shirt on top of the mattress. "I kept it for you."

Julian takes the shirt and puts it on.

"You left in such a hurry the other day. You all right?"

Julian doesn't answer.

The horn shrieks. He now has five minutes to use the latrines, five to wash up, and five to eat. Things will come one by one, in their own time, so he convinces himself.

39

Four Sundays later, he sleeps most of the morning, misses breakfast, then late in the afternoon, he takes a shower and walks about the grounds. Behind the shower area, he sits underneath the shade of an almond tree. The day's brightness seems, in the same lazy manner he spent his childhood Sundays, to demand nothing but repose and relaxation.

A wild dove flies from one tree, chased by two sparrows, to the water canal of the showers. Fermin, he heard, got into a fight with the soldier who double-crossed him and was put back into the cell. Wondering when Fermin will be released, he drowses only to be awakened hours later by cheers, which seem to be coming from the hills, where everything appears to have gone up in flames.

"Fight!" a man says, running past Julian.

Julian runs and catches up with the man. "What happened?" he asks.

"A fight broke out in the hills," the man says between breaths "Orlando's fighting a *guajiro.*"

Everything darkens as he runs. When they get to the foothills, the man leaves Julian behind. He vanishes into the circle of men holding torches, shouting and booing. The men on the outside jump up in order to see. Julian climbs a tree. The thick bark scrapes his hands and knees. In the center of the circle, a barebacked man in torn pants holding a knife is trying to cut Orlando.

"Cut your balls off, *cabrón,*" the man shouts. "Teach you to respect a man's wife."

"And a fine wife she is," Orlando says. Everybody laughs, and this angers the man into a swinging frenzy.

Orlando, whose back is scratched, remains silent. Like a boxer, he guards his face and stomach with his forearms and fists. Whenever the man swings his arm and tries to cut Orlando, the crowd boos.

Stepping back, Orlando stumbles and falls. He stands quickly and charges.

"Come on. Give him all you got. Throw it at him!" someone shouts in the crowd.

"Use this," another man says. A stick lands on the ground by Orlando's feet, then another is thrown to the other man.

The smacking of the sticks hitting flesh and bones echoes. Orlando moves, and then strikes again. This attack and retreat continues until the man manages to sneak in a blow to Orlando's leg. Orlando falls and rolls on his side. The man hits him twice on the side of the head before the stick cracks and breaks.

The man is upon Orlando now, hitting him.

A shot comes from the dark woods, silencing the crowd. Some of the men run away.

"Break it up!" the sergeant shouts. "I want the man responsible for this!" He makes his way through the parting circle to the two men in the center. The sergeant orders them to be taken away, then he shouts at everyone to return to camp immediately. "Move!"

The men run downhill.

Julian hesitates to jump from the branch. He has failed to realize how high he has climbed. The sergeant follows the soldiers. After they disappear, Julian slides down the trunk and runs back to camp before Leandro locks him out of the barracks.

40

For weeks no one mentions the incident. Julian manages to overhear that Orlando is in detention in the barracks where he'd been. In midafternoon the carts, pulled by two pairs of oxen, come to pick up the bundles of cane and take them to the mill.

Dark clouds move across the sky and cover the sun, but it doesn't rain until the trucks return to pick up the cutters. The canvas tops have been removed. When it begins to rain, the cutters cheer, and suddenly the sound of the machetes is replaced by the rain falling.

Most of the men take their shirts off. "This must be a gift from God," says one man, looking up at the sky, and then holds his tongue out. Another man does the same, but closes his eyes. Rain falls over everything: carts, oxen, cane bundles, piles of boots and machetes, and ground.

At least now, Julian thinks, the rain'll wash the charcoal off the stalks.

"Look," the man next to Julian says to another, pointing to the slanted smoke coming out of the mill's smokestacks. "They're determined, aren't they?"

Arriving at camp, even before the trucks come to a complete stop, the men jump out and run to the barracks. The water falls upon the drivers' uniforms. Julian follows with his shirt in his hand.

"All the water we need," a man says, dancing in the overflowing water trough with his pants rolled up his skinny legs. "Holy water."

A cutter approaches Julian and warns him to be careful with Leandro.

41

Fermin, who is finally released, looks skinnier. Julian speaks to him during breaks, and when the trucks take them to and from the fields. "What being locked up can do to a man," he tells Julian. Julian asks him if he has seen Orlando, but Fermin says he hadn't.

Three days later Julian writes Carmina. He sends her the money he was paid for last month's work, eighty-five pesos. He tries to avoid Leandro at all times.

The following nights the fields burn. By dawn, the gray smoke hovers like fog over the burned cane. The cutting becomes unbearable in so much heat. The earth is burning, Julian thinks. One night at three o'clock in the morning, the horns awake everybody. Leandro runs inside the barracks and tells everyone that a fire has spread and is headed toward the camp.

The machetes and boots change hands fast outside, then the sleepy cutters are driven to the fire. A voice orders a wide ditch to be dug only feet away from where the fire consumes the cane. Reddening the night, the flames rise and turn in huge orange whorls. Spirals. Julian wants the fire to burn the camp down to ashes.

But eventually the fire is controlled. By seven everyone heads back to camp to eat breakfast and get ready to start cutting again.

"If this isn't slavery," a man says, "then I'm out of tune with reality."

"Not much work'll get done today," adds another man.

"Tired men don't produce."

"For them every cane cut is one step closer to the magic number."

"Ten million."

Five Mig-15s fly in V formation overhead, slicing through the scattered clouds. Not even the sonic boom manages to startle Julian as he slouches from the truck to the mess hall.

42

Names are called from a list. The men the soldier calls gather in a semicircle while the whispers of their conversations subside during calls. "Campos!" the soldier calls.

Julian walks over to where all the men stand. Some of them seem a bit nervous.

"Follow me," the soldier says, folding the list and securing it on the clipboard.

The cutters get ready to go to the fields. Julian follows the line to the truck. "Where are we headed?" he asks the man in front.

"Don't you know?" the man says, not turning. "To the mill."

Julian has never been to one. In Oriente he had only cut cane. "What for?"

"Wait and see."

He climbs in, sits, and rests his elbows on the tailgate.

"Look," the man sitting next to Julian says, pointing.

Everyone looks. Up in the driver's compartment, behind the glass, a guard dog turns its white fangs to the glass.

"Why the goddamned dog?" someone from the back wants to know.

"To make sure we get to our destination."

Down the middle of the road, the fields meet at the vanishing point. The tires leave wavy prints on the soft mud. The fields run out, and now the truck drives along telephone poles, which shrink in the distance. Julian counts them as he once did when he was small and his parents would take him out for a drive. The more poles he counted, the more candies his father bought him at the ice-cream parlor in downtown Cienfuegos. The truck passes a man on horseback.

"How do carts get to the mill?"

"Take a shortcut. That road's too narrow for this truck."

A black woman wearing a faded green dress with an orange scarf turbaned on her head appears. She carries two baskets of laundry, one under each arm, while her child skips next to her. He raises his hands when the truck passes and waves, but stops when she looks down and tells him something.

The truck slows down and goes by a sentry booth, then by an open gate, and finally it drives down an asphalt road. When the truck stops. everyone jumps out of the back and regroups. The men are led by the driver inside the oversized warehouse. In it pipes hiss and tubes gurgle. Combines grind. Steam blows toward the high ceiling, from which huge air vents hang. As soon as he enters through the giant iron doors the sweet smell of processed cane comes to him. Machinery shrieks and turns and chug-chugs and jerks. The cutting and grinding noises echo loudest by the entrance, drowning the voices of men.

"Keep it moving!" someone shouts from behind.

A man wearing faded khakis and a T-shirt comes to the group and speaks to the driver. He sends the men in different directions. "You, come with me," he says to Julian.

The man leads him through narrow passageways between pipes of different widths and sizes that emit heat. Cane floats down a canal of dark water. Toward the other side of the building, dozens of men lift and carry sacks on their shoulders They stack them on top of pallets. Once they reach the outside, Julian can see the sky and fields once again. Fresh air, sunlight, and the intensity of the noise diminishes. Here carts wait to be unloaded. "Work here," the man tells him. He pulls his handkerchief out of his back pocket and wipes the sweat off the back of his neck and forehead. "Put the bundles on top of the conveyor belt. Simple, no?" He points to the moving bundles.

Julian approaches the ox carts where six or seven men sweat, unloading, and imitating their actions, he picks up two bundles at a time and drops them on top of the belt. Simple. Just before finishing his first cart, another arrives.

By midafternoon, he picks up only one bundle at a time, with both hands. He doesn't stop for lunch since no one else stops and since no one comes to instruct him to do so. After a long while, after he loses count of how many carts he has unloaded, he feels certain that he won't get a rest. So he works at an even slower pace. But the carts keep coming and he wonders where the hell so many of them keep coming from.

43

More carts arrive and Julian tries to recognize any of the oxen, which swat the flies off their rumps while they chew cud in a contemplative fashion. He slams the bundles hard against the belt, which rattles, but doesn't stop. Rest, he tells himself, relax. The man nearest to him, who has kept busy all day, looks at him and smiles. He has been working now for twelve hours, maybe more.

The night hides the fields. A whistle blows twice. The man who led Julian here comes and tells him to hurry up, that the truck is waiting for him. Julian wants to pick the bastard up and throw him on the belt. He imagines the man's bones being ground somewhere inside the mill.

At the camp, dinner is about over by the time he showers and gets dressed. On his way out of the barracks, Leandro stops him.

"What do you want?" Julian asks.

"You're jumpy, man. From tomorrow on everyone goes to bathe in the river," Leandro says.

Julian remains silent.

"The camp's well ran out."

Julian doesn't say anything and walks outside, where he meets Fermin. Fermin, when Julian tells him, laughs. When he stops laughing, he asks Julian how he's feeling.

"Very tired."

"Where do you think they've been keeping me all this time?"

Julian can't guess.

"The mill." Fermin eats with gusto as though he hasn't eaten in a long time.

"Know what?" Fermin says, lowering his voice. "Someone's going to get me some *aguardiente.*"

"You've forgotten what happened last time," Julian says.

"Nothing like that's going to happen. This person knows how to trade with *guajiros.* They make it out of rice, you know, or cane. Anyway, he's going to get me a couple of bottles."

"Who is he?"

"Classified information."

"How much is it going to cost you?"

"Fifty."

"Fifty? That's almost a month's pay, Fermin."

"So what? What do I need money here for?"

"Send it to your wife. Or Ofelia."

"Silvia doesn't want my money."

"Don't drink it away."

"No lectures, okay?"

"It'll kill you."

"It's not the drinking that's going to kill me. Besides, I'd like to die drunk. What better way is there. Maybe making love to a fine woman, you know." He laughs.

"How do you know this isn't another trick?"

"This time it's legitimate. This man's not a soldier or anything of the sort. He's got authority."

"But it could still be a trick."

"I don't hand over the money until I'm in possession of the merchandise."

"What if you get caught?"

"I get caught I get caught," he says.

After Julian finishes eating, he walks outside with Fermin. They walk back to the barracks in complete silence. Dogs bark behind the sergeant's barracks. Inside, over his bunk, he finds Orlando snoring.

44

Before sundown the cutters are driven to the river, which hides like broken pieces of mirror beyond the cane fields. Julian splashes water on his chest and back, then submerges to clean his face and get the soot out of his hair. The black substance dissolves into rings around him. Quick ripples crawl over the sandy edges of the river and lick at the tips of the submerged rocks and boulders.

"This must be a great place to fish," Orlando says, coming out of the water, dripping. He walks over the dry ground and sits down next to Fermin, who lies on his back.

"Perhaps there aren't any fish in there," Fermin says.

"It's still a good place."

"What good is it if there are no fish."

"How do you know?"

"I'm only saying. Maybe they died."

"Well, if there were any, this would be a good place to fish," Orlando says, sitting on his heels. "See that spot over there? I'd go there and fish. Under the shade of those trees."

"Have you done much fishing?"

"All the time. But not in recent years. When I was a boy, I loved to fish."

"I fished every day for ten years. A river like this one ran through the backyard of my parents' house."

"What made you stop?"

"What made us all stop?"

The drivers appear to be involved in a long conversation. They sit or stand against the front fender of the nearest truck. Orlando, who keeps looking at the drivers, tells Fermin one of his stories about how a Spanish cavalryman raped a woman's daughter during the War of Independence. Immediately after the horns blow, Orlando dives into the river. Julian waits for him to resurface, but he doesn't, not until he is on the other side.

Everyone hurries out of the water, their clothes sticking to their skins. Fermin pushes himself up off the ground, leaving a wet mark of his body imprinted on the dirt. The sun descends and only its trail of orange remains in the sky. Before the trucks drive away, Julian looks at the water sparkling one last time. Fermin winks at him. On the other side of the river, the blue of the night chases the orange into the horizon.

45

The following night footsteps approach in the dark. On his side, Julian faces the wall of the barracks. He feels his mattress sink as though someone has sat on it. He rolls over and bumps against a body.

"Sssh!" the voice says. "Keep quiet. It's me, Leandro."

Julian sits up. "What the hell are you doing on my bed?"

"How would you like to buy some *aguardiente*?"

Julian pushes him off. Leandro sits on the bed again. "I'll take you to the hills to a pretty—"

"Get off," Julian says, standing. He thinks that this must have been the way Fermin got caught.

Leandro's sweaty hand touches Julian's arm. "How about it?"

Julian grabs Leandro by the neck and pulls him up.

"You'll wake everybody up."

There are shadows sitting upright on the bunks. Julian folds his fingers into a fist, swings, and hits Leandro's jaw. His knuckles crack as though each one has shattered into a million pieces. Leandro staggers backward, then falls on the dirt floor. "Get up!"

He gets up slowly, shakes his head, and once again stands in front of Julian. Julian strikes, but Leandro blocks the punch and kicks Julian's thigh with his heel. Julian turns and lets Leandro have one under the rib cage.

"Fight!" someone shouts.

"Stop, you'll both get in trouble," Fermin says, stepping in from behind.

Leandro hits Julian below his left eye. Fermin pulls Leandro outside. Everyone returns to their bunks. Julian grows calm as he hears Leandro threatening Fermin.

46

At sunrise a soldier shakes Julian awake and tells him that the sergeant wants to see him. The sergeant is sitting behind his desk when Julian walks in.

"What am I to do with you, Campos?"

"What happened last night wasn't my fault," Julian says.

"Yes. I've heard the whole story."

"Not from me."

"It seems you have a hard time controlling your temper," the sergeant says.

"All I want is to be left alone to do the job I was brought out here to do."

"You'll be left alone. Watch your conduct from now on. I have my men keeping their eyes on you. I want no more trouble, understand?"

"Christ, Leandro was the one trafficking and—"

"He won't bother anyone again. I've transferred him to another camp. Remember, Campos, one more from you and you'll be cutting cane for a long while."

47

Dogs bark and sniff on top of Orlando's mattress, then they are taken outside and released. A day later, they return. One of them limps. There's dry blood on the fur under its belly.

Another month passes. The river water turns muddy after a week of rains. The men appear not to be too concerned with the water as long as they get to go to the river after work. A full beard covers Julian's face for the first time in his life. He receives a letter from Carmina. Things have changed, she writes, you'll see for yourself when you come.

During the middle of the month, he learns shocking news. Fermin died one night, drunk, so they said. The sergeant refuses to give details. Fermin died drunk. If these facts mean anything, they mean that he died happy, he thinks. The body is sent to Habana for an autopsy. Julian writes Carmina telling her the bad news, although he knows that by the time his letter reaches her, she will have attended the wake, funeral, and burial.

The Ten-Million-Ton program, according to the men who gossip, has failed. Only seven million tons have been cut. The sergeant withdraws out of sight, but as punishment, he increases the work pace. The days become longer, the rest periods shorter, and Sunday's rest is replaced by more cutting By now everyone seems to know that no matter how hard they work, the program has failed. Julian slows his pace.

And still more good things happen: The torrential rains begin. The rain falls so hard that by the end of the month all work in the fields stops. Julian hears that a cyclone is believed to be under way.

On the last day of cutting, a man finds Orlando's head. The eyes on the deformed face have been nibbled away by ants. The man who found the head disappears. Some of the men say that he was sent to the mill in Matanzas.

48

Friday morning a soldier walks out of the rain and into the barracks. He approaches Julian's bunk under close scrutiny from the rest of the cutters and says that the sergeant wants to see him immediately. What does he want this time? Julian wonders as he runs to the barracks. He finds the sergeant standing by the window.

"What do you want?" Julian asks.

The sergeant moves away from the window without replying, opens the top drawer of his desk, picks an envelope out, and throws it on top of the desk. "They want you back in Habana," he says.

The excitement grows, so that Julian can't help smiling.

"Drive him to the station," the sergeant tells the soldier by the door.

The soldier opens the door and follows Julian under the rain. "The truck's over there," he says.

Julian runs fast.

"You can ride in front."

Holding the envelope under his shirt, Julian runs around to the side door, opens it, and climbs inside. The soldier starts the motor. The windshield wipers sweep the drops away as quickly as they fall. The truck drives away from the barracks, and past the barbed-wire fence. In the side mirror, everything blurs under the downpour.

49

El Lechero, as the station attendant calls the train, arrives late. Julian climbs the two steps and tries to squeeze in through some of the bodies. He holds on to the handrails, while half of his torso hangs out. As the train moves out from under the ledge he thinks that surely someone has to get off at the next station or he will never make it to Habana. The rain makes the handrails slippery. A man holding a sack stands next to him. After the train makes a stop and more room becomes available. the man puts the sack on the step and sits. "We finally get a breather," he says.

Julian sits down next to him. There is hardly any light coming through to see his face clearly.

"Where are you going?" the man asks.

"Habana."

"Taking this to my kids," he says.

"What's in it?"

"Rice. I couldn't stand the sight of them having to go hungry."

"How many do you have?"

"Two. A boy and a girl. I would be in trouble if I had more. These two can eat for four." The man breaks into a laugh, as though he remembers something. "Do you have children?" he continues.

Julian says no.

"That's too bad. Kids are wonderful. My kids are the reason why I'm still around."

The rain falls slanted and wets the sack. The man puts his hands out and washes his face.

Camacho, as the man introduces himself, falls asleep with his head against the metal of the entrance. His eyes twitch every time drops fall on them. Relaxed by the swaying motion of the wagon on the tracks, Julian dozes off. The train takes a sharp curve and veers. The sack comes loose from Camacho's grip. The sudden movement startles him, as though he thinks someone is stealing his rice. The sack tears in the middle and most of the rice spills. The rain washes it away over the edge of the steps.

"Please help me pick it up," he says.

Julian helps him before all of it vanishes. He scoops up a lot of it, but it's no use: most of it falls. "I m sorry," he tells Camacho.

"It isn't your fault. I'm stupid," he says, still collecting. What little rice remains in the sack, he puts behind him. "I went all the way to La Cienega de Zapata for nothing." Camacho hits his thigh with his fist. Julian sits under the rain next to him; the man bends his arms over his knees and hides his face.

The Operation

50

The bad news, Carmina reveals the morning Julian arrives, is that his house was given to a party member's family. She argued to no avail with the officers who came to take inventory, but the house, they told her, belongs to the government. She managed, though, to sneak out all of Bernarda's belongings. Now a party member and his family occupy the house.

The following day, after he rests, Julian, sitting on the brick fence that divides Carmina's house from his, sees what has happened. His house has been painted, all the cages dismantled, and the wood stacked in a corner of the patio.

"Ready to go?" Carmina says to him from the kitchen doorway.

"Where?" Julian says, jumping down from the fence.

"To the cemetery," she says. "I want you to see her grave."

"There can be no other explanation," he says. "They're going to grant me the exit."

She assures him it seems that way. As they walk up the street away from Fermin's house, she suggests that he go over and offer Silvia and Ofelia condolences. Fermin's death from a heart attack, she says, came as a shock to them. She gives Julian a plastic sheet to use as cover in case it rains.

"How do you like my son's bed?" she asks.

"It's comfortable," he says.

Nicanor stands against his doorway and stares as Carmina and Julian pass by. Carmina waves at him and he waves back.

SUPPORT A NEW REVOLUTION! DEATH TO THE PARTY PIGS! and STOP SLAVERY! cover the outside wall of the cemetery's entrance. Julian opens the iron gate for Carmina. Wall to wall, thumb-like, sticking out of the wet earth, tombstones crowd the narrow walkway. Carmina stops in front of a stoneless grave.

"Here," she says, and looks down.

"Why doesn't she have a tombstone?"

"The caretaker, he told me weeks ago that as soon as he gets—"

"My grandmother must have a tombstone."

Julian kneels, searches around for a stick with which to scratch the ground, finds a dry rose stem, and writes BERNARDA DEL RIO, 1895-1969.

Drops fall and soak the soft earth while the scratches fade slowly.

"We'll get flowers as soon as it stops raining," he says.

"No flowers," she says. "They get stolen."

The rain taps hard on the plastic while he holds it over her head as they hurry down the cobblestone road. Julian repeats to himself that he won't die here.

51

Ofelia opens the door and seems not to recognize Julian. He thinks of his untrimmed beard that covers his thin lips. Her breasts look fuller hidden under the ruffles of the peach blouse she's wearing. She doesn't look consumed, as he expected, but content. He asks her if her mother's home.

"When did you get here?" Ofelia asks.

"Yesterday."

"The beard makes you look older. A lot different."

"I'll shave it if it makes me a stranger."

"Not a stranger, no. I think it looks good." She smiles. "Come in, I'll call her," she says.

She hurries into another room and gently closes the door behind her. Julian sits facing the drawn, dusty-looking curtains of the living-room window. From the kitchen comes the soft buzzing of the refrigerator.

Suddenly the door opens and Silvia and Ofelia walk out.

"Julian," Silvia says. "Don't get up." A crackle of excitement in her voice makes it seem like she is receiving a close friend or relative.

"I thought I'd come." He takes her hand and squeezes it, then he tells her how sorry he is about Fermin.

She smiles and the skin around her mouth wrinkles as her lips crook upward. He lets go of her hand and, at her gesture, sits on the worn divan.

"Oh, and your grandmother—I'm sure that must have been difficult," she says, sitting on the easy chair, "but one has to deal with such circumstances." Ofelia carries a chair from the kitchen, sets it down slowly, and sits next to her mother.

He tells Silvia what friends Fermin and he became in the fields. While he speaks, he notices Ofelia staring at him. Her eyes have a sparkle of interest in them.

"He told me all about the troubles you went through in his letters," Silvia says. "He wasn't a bad man, but when he turned to alcohol, him and me stopped being husband and wife."

Julian looks at Ofelia, who in turn looks at her hands. which rest on her thighs.

"Always drank. Even before we were engaged, but not as much and not such terrible liquor."

"I think he drank because he felt helpless." *Hopeless?*

"Is that what he told you?"

"Once. I sensed it in the way he spoke about his disillusionment. Carmina told me he died of a heart attack."

"That's what the coroner who performed the autopsy told me."

Ofelia sighs, and her breasts, large like her mother's, push against the confinement of the silk. Her hands rest palms-up on her lap. He fights the urge to mention Orlando, but Silvia interrupts him by asking if he wants a glass of lemonade. He says water will be fine. Silvia stands and walks to the kitchen, Although she has white hair and the skin on her face is wrinkled, she manages to keep a youthful poise.

The refrigerator door clicks open. Shut. Ice cubes chink as they fall into a glass in the kitchen. Julian sits quietly in front of Ofelia, looking at the way her large eyes remain still.

"Carmina tells me you're leaving soon?" Ofelia asks. "It is true, isn't it."

He tells her yes, he hopes. "You sound interested."

"More than you think," she says, and turns to the kitchen. Her eyes narrow under her bushy eyebrows. "We are leaving. too."

"I didn't know you had applied for the exit. Your father didn't—"

"We didn't. My mother knows—" She stops, looks at the kitchen again, and draws closer. "She knows a group that is leaving by boat. A boat from Caracas—"

Silvia brings a tray with two glasses of lemonade into the living room. "I hope it's sweet enough," she says.

"Mother, he wanted water."

"Tell me if it needs more sugar."

He sips the cold liquid. A piece of ice gets in the way of the flow and stings his front teeth. "Hmmm, it's good," he says.

"Mother oversweetens everything," Ofelia says.

Silvia laughs. "That's not so."

Julian looks at Ofelia, not convinced by the information she has revealed. Silvia might know, but if he asks her about it, Ofelia might get into trouble.

He drinks fast, hoping Silvia'll give them a few more moments alone. When he finishes, Ofelia stands and takes the glass from his hands. He fights the urge to signal her to stay, to let Silvia take the glasses to the kitchen.

"Would you like more?" Ofelia asks, putting the glass down on top of the coffee table.

He tells her no. "Thanks, but I better go. Carmina has dinner ready."

"Do you play dominoes, Julian?" Silvia asks. "We'd love to have you over sometime."

"I haven't played in a long time."

"Dominoes is an easy game," Ofelia says, holding her arms as though she were cold. "You'll remember after two hands." She turns and gives the glass to her mother, who says good-bye and goes to the kitchen.

Ofelia walks Julian to the door, reaches for the knob but doesn't open the door.

"Listen to how hard it is raining," he says.

She cracks the door open.

The rain slaps on the fronds of the *palmeras* by the side of the porch. They both step onto the wet tiles, then Julian bends over and picks up his piece of plastic. "Carmina's idea," he says, and smiles.

She turns to look behind her, then, keeping the door shut, she says, "Return during the blackout and I'll tell you about the operation."

52

Any of the windows could be Ofelia's. In the dark he takes his chances, squats, and taps with his fingertips on the glass. What if the curtains part and Silvia's face appears? He feels his breath on his dry lips.

Hands move under the curtains and pull the window open. "Sssh! My mother's still awake," Ofelia says.

Julian removes his shoes so he won't leave mud anywhere and climbs in carefully. Her bedsprings squeak when he steps onto her mattress.

"This is crazy," he says, a little nervous and out of breath.

"Don't worry, my mother's room is on the other side. She'll fall asleep soon. Can't stand to be up during blackouts."

A candle burns on top of the dresser behind Ofelia, whose body shows through her nightgown.

"Don't get the wrong impression," she says, sitting on top of her bed and resting her feet up on the edge of the dresser.

"Don't burn your toes," she says, reaching over and moving the flame away from her feet. "I've asked you here for one reason. Carmina has told me how hard they've treated you."

"You've talked to her?"

"A couple of times. I ran into her at the bodega. Don't you know?"

"What?" he says, crossing his arms.

"I always ask her about you."

"You do."

"I want you to know about the boat from Caracas just in case—" She stops and looks at the candle.

"Go on."

"What if they won't let you go?"

"Oh, they will. I mean they have to."

"They don't have to, you should know that by now."

Her breathless, dead tone of voice gets him angry. "I'll find out tomorrow," he says.

"Screw them."

"That's a no-no."

"Don't trust them."

"I never have, but this time I have to believe that they'll let me go," he says, and avoids looking down her thighs. "Anyway, you've seen what they did with the house."

"That doesn't mean anything." Ofelia pats the space next to her for him to sit down.

"It means something to me. Besides, Carmina believes it, too." He sits next to her.

"Come on, Julian, you can't rely on Carmina's silly hunches."

"It's not a silly hunch."

"Keep it down," she says, and puts her fingers across his lips.

"Fine then, what's the alternative?"

"The boat coming from Caracas will take us to Florida. The group leader hasn't revealed the exact date and time."

"How much?"

"Five hundred dollars."

"That's a lot."

"Carmina might have it," she says.

"How many people?"

"There are six groups of four to five people . . ."

Julian thinks he hears a heel tap on the floorboards. "God, I do hope they let you leave." Ofelia puts her hand on his knee, but withdraws it immediately.

"This is crazy," he says. "I better go before the streetlights come back on. The last thing I want's for somebody to catch me coming out of your window."

"No one's going to see you."

"Let's talk about this after tomorrow."

"At what time do you have to be at the Ministry of the Interior?"

"Between eight and nine."

"Come back some other night?" she says.

"Soon."

"Promise."

"You've got to tell me the rest, right?"

"Whatever you want to know," she says, and takes his hand, "but after tomorrow I hope you have no use for any of it."

On impulse he stands up, climbs out of her room, and slips his shoes back on. Biting her bottom lip, she gently lowers the window, then makes an "okay" sign with her fingers. He returns the gesture, then, in the dark, runs like a startled cat across the street.

53

The manila file splits open to reveal a piece of notepaper clipped to the corner. Nothing more, nothing less. A note. The man picks up the note and reads: "Papers have been transferred to military headquarters for reevaluation."

"Military headquarters. Surely that's a mistake," Julian says.

"Wait until further notice," the man says. "Or get in touch with them directly. In the meantime report to Polar Brewery. You'll get a position there."

"Shit. I've waited too long, long enough! Too long for this. I don't want to work. I want to leave. Leave!"

"Control yourself."

"Are you sure that's mine?"

"Campos," the man says, showing Julian his typewritten name on the label, then closes the file and walks away.

"Son of a bitch!" Julian says to his back. A few sticks of dynamite, he thinks as he hurries down the narrow flight of stairs, placed in the right corners, and the building will turn to dust and rubble.

54

What his father did troubles Julian on the way home, brings back recollections of difficult times. He remembers the nights his father comes home from Polar Brewery, drunk, in a stupor, and fills the dark house with screams while Bernarda tries to appease him. One night Julian hears his mother scream from the living room from where music plays on the radio, and when he runs barefoot in his pajamas out of his room, he finds the living-room walls on fire, flames and smoke everywhere. His grandmother and mother rush to the kitchen to get water. The front door is wide open, and all Julian sees are the leaves of the banana plants swaying in the dark of the porch.

55

The ball of yarn rolls on Carmina's lap every time she pulls more slack. "They've turned me back for the last time," he says, entering the room and leaning against the wall.

"Chango have mercy!"

While he tells her everything, Carmina keeps her eyes closed. "I'll go to jail before reenlisting . . . I'm leaving, Carmina. Leaving . . . clandestinely. With Silvia and Ofelia."

"You found out?"

"You knew about the operation?"

"I didn't want you to get involved . . . I thought this time . . ." she says. "It's dangerous, Julian. You don't—"

"My mind's made up. Tonight I'll talk to Silvia."

"You'll risk getting caught."

"I'll take the risk."

"Think about it."

"I'm tired of thinking. It's time to act. No one knows about it."

"That's what you don't know."

He leaves her room and goes to Andres's room, where he sits and thinks about his options. They leave him with no other choice but to get away, somehow. Only, God knows, he doesn't want to go anywhere but America. He thinks until his mind boggles and tires.

On top of the chiffonier, by a picture of Andres wearing his first-private uniform, shy smile on his lips, he spots Bernarda's Harvard edition of the *Thousand and One Nights,* opens it, and reads until the blackout.

56

A sudden breeze hisses through the blades of the miniature *palmeras* by the side of Fermin's porch. The sky has turned to a dark ash color. The second Ofelia opens the door, he tells her he wants to see her mother.

"They won't let you go, huh?" she says.

"It's up to your mother," he tells her.

"She's in the shower. Why don't you let me talk to her. I can persuade her. Come to my window later and I'll tell you what she says."

"Explain it to her. Tell her they're going to make me reenlist."

"She listens to me."

Silvia walks up behind Ofelia in her bathrobe. "What's the matter, Julian?"

He tells her what happened.

"That's horrible. What will you do?"

He tells her he's got no other alternative.

"Can't your parents do anything through the consulate?"

"Who knows?"

"Mother, I don't think there's much he can do," Ofelia says. "He's running out of time." She mentions something about hope and faith, but he isn't listening. He thinks he hears thunder in the distance.

Silvia excuses herself to go dry her hair and change. He stays on the porch with Ofelia, who reassures him that her mother will say yes. She takes his hand out of his pocket and squeezes it.

There is a pause while they sit on the porch steps. All around is darkness. Dogs bark far away.

"I remember when you first moved here," Ofelia says. "I spent my time waiting by the window for you to pass . . . or come out to play. You often played, remember? On the plank you built across Carmina's roof and yours . . . you'd sit there for hours. What did you pretend you were doing?

"I envied you so much. I was never allowed to play the way you did. No . . . Father never let me. Instead I sat inside. Bored. I had to listen to them argue all the time." She stops and looks away beyond the *palmeras.*

"But the day the bus came to pick you up and take you to camp, I was outside. You didn't see me by the side of the house, or did you? Mother called me inside the moment she saw the bus. Then you were gone for three years.

"Whenever mother ran into Carmina at the bodega, I'd always ask her about you and she'd always say you were all right."

"I wasn't all right, but I was surviving," he says. "I tried to follow orders so that I wouldn't get into trouble. They tried their best to brainwash me, you know, but they couldn't. Sometimes I followed orders so that they'd leave me alone."

"Must have been lonely."

"If I don't risk it and leave with you now, now that I have the chance, I'll have to spend more time in uniform. You know, sometimes I wish I'd have been born under the system. I figure if you don't know better, you'd be able to accept it as it is. I'd be flawless. But I know there's got to be a better way to live. There's got to be, otherwise, why even bother to leave? Maybe if I had never known my parents, if my grandmother had died while I was still a child, I would be a captain in the army today. Imagine that, me a captain." He laughs.

"I have to go," Ofelia says, stands, and smoothes the wrinkles on her skirt.

He watches her go inside and then stays on the porch for a moment. Thunder rolls. He feels a slight pang on his forehead. He shivers. While the rain falls he walks slowly under it and wishes that a lightning bolt would split him in two.

In the house he drips water on the floor of Andres's room while Carmina takes his temperature and tells him to rest. He changes into dry clothes, climbs into bed, and after moments of being alone in the silence of the room a violent fever overpowers him and takes him deep into unconsciousness.

57

"Pray to God for the daily bread you are about to eat!" Julian's Young Pioneer battalion leader says from the entrance of the cafeteria. His military stance and the way his beady eyes always seem to carry a smile of mockery had seeded a deep hatred in Julian.

By now everyone knows the outcome of these words. No one prays, or makes the slightest motion to.

"Now ask your party's leader for your daily bread!"

After a short-lived silence, everyone asks.

The battalion leader orders the food to be brought. Carts appear from behind the kitchen door, then the food is distributed evenly among the pale faces between shrieks and laughter.

58

"How are you feeling?" he hears Carmina say, then turns in her direction. Wearing an emerald-green scarf on her head, she sits next to him with a pail on her lap in which she rinses a face towel. There is a thick smell of jasmine in the room. The water feels cool on his forehead as it drips down on his face.

"I've defeated your fever," she says.

"How long have I been like this? I have to see Ofelia."

"It's noon. You've been out for sixteen hours. Take care of yourself. Colds are treacherous. They return the moment they detect weakness."

"Nothing from Silvia?"

"Ofelia came by this morning. She told me she has good news, but wants to give it to you herself. She said for you to go over."

Carmina picks up the pail, holds it steady with both hands, and walks slowly to the door.

Though his beard itches and he feels sticky and unclean, he wastes no time in getting dressed and going to Fermin's house. The air feels crisp against his warm skin. There, someone he can't see in the dark lets him in. He feels as though he is intruding. Ghostlike, the figure lights the candle. "Who are you?" he asks.

"Blancarosa."

Julian cannot believe her. She doesn't seem to recognize him. "Remember me?" he asks.

She looks at him for a while, under the light. "No," she says finally.

"Campos, I sat next to you Olivo's history class." At first she doesn't respond but then says, "It's been a long time. Whatever happened to you?"

"Cutting cane in Perseverancia."

Silvia's door opens and Ofelia walks out. "Are you feeling better?" Ofelia says.

"Much."

Blancarosa moves back to let Ofelia pass. She walks up to Julian as though she is going to hug him. "Did you meet Blancarosa?"

He nods.

"Come to the bedroom," Silvia's voice comes from her room.

Julian follows Blancarosa. The house is filled with the aroma of burned wax. Ofelia places the *candelero* on the center of the bed. The three women gather around the bed, on their knees. Blancarosa and Silvia on the other side. Julian sits with his legs crossed under him next to Ofelia, who taps his thigh and smiles. He looks at the darkness of Blancarosa's eyes under the cast of the flame's flicker.

"Julian joined recently," Silvia tells Blancarosa.

"They know each other," Ofelia says.

"Another time, another place," says Blancarosa.

"It's better this way," Silvia says.

Julian shrugs, still puzzled by Blancarosa's involvement in the operation, for the last time he had seen her was with a lieutenant. Silvia and Blancarosa go over the details of the plan. "No one can be late," Silvia says. "Every minute counts. The boat'll pick us up at three-thirty at Cabo Hicacos."

"Word from Caracas," Blancarosa says, "assures us that there'll be enough room on the boat. Do you have the money?"

Julian says Carmina will lend it to him. "What kind of boat is it?" Julian asks.

"Fishing," Blancarosa answers. "It'll hide behind Cayo Blancos and send a launch to the point."

Blancarosa's job involves going from group to group with information of the latest changes. Silvia is in charge of the groups. Since Blancarosa is one of the drivers, she asks him to ride with her. Ofelia suggests that he ride with her and her mother, but Silvia ignores her request. Each car will leave Habana one hour after the last. Ofelia grows serious, her cheeks orange.

"It's all set," Silvia says, standing. "Monday next week. We leave Sunday night."

"That should be enough time to regroup on the beach," Blancarosa says.

"Why don't you make us coffee, Ofe?" Silvia says.

Ofelia carries out the candle, sets it on the center table, and disappears into the kitchen, where she rattles pots and pans.

"I had figured you differently," he says to Blancarosa. "What became of your boyfriend, the lieutenant?"

"Lieutenant?"

"Forgot him already, huh?"

Blancarosa holds a steady smile on her lips. "He was my brother's friend," she says. "That day he came to tell me that my brother had been killed in Matanzas."

"How?"

She tells him the party refuses to reveal how. All they keep telling her is that her brother was involved in a security-type drill when he lost his life. She had encouraged him to join the army, believing that it was the only way her brother would survive. "Some of us pretend better than others," she says. "That's how I survive. I'm a good . . . All my life I've done all that is asked of me. I don't ask questions. I do. If you manage to do that, then you survive . . . you live. I could stay and have everything I want, but I can't stay. You'd expect them to be straightforward about my brother's death."

Ofelia returns from the kitchen with two cups of steaming coffee.

"I'm sorry, Silvia, but I have to leave before the lights return," Blancarosa says.

"Me too," he says. hoping to be alone with Blancarosa.

"Keep in touch with me throughout the week," Silvia says.

He watches Blancarosa's lips pucker around the rim of the porcelain cup. "Thank you," she says, then hands Ofelia, who looks at Julian with a blank look on her face, the empty cup.

"I'll talk to you later," he says to Ofelia.

Julian follows Blancarosa to the porch, where he opens the largest piece of plastic and raises it over her head. "Get under," he tells her. Ofelia closes the door without saying good-bye.

Blancarosa holds on to his arm as he walks her to the corner. "I think she's upset with you," she says.

"Ofelia?"

"Who else?"

"How can you tell?"

"For another woman it's easy to tell," she says, and smiles.

"I don't have the slightest idea what could be the matter."

"I get the feeling she likes you. I saw the way she was looking at you all the time we were talking."

"It's hard to think of someone you've known most of your life that way."

"Which way?"

"In terms of liking or disliking, you either do or you don't. I think she's a very nice girl."

"So you like her," Blancarosa says.

They fall silent for a brief moment, then Julian breaks it by saying, "That last day you saw me I was going to ask you out."

"Why didn't you?"

"I had my doubts about you."

"That's funny, I had serious ones about you. Are you sure about me now?"

"Why don't you take me up on my offer?"

"I just might. How about if I come visit you. Where are you staying?"

He points to the dark facade of Carmina's house. "When will you come?"

"Soon. They are keeping me busy."

"Who?"

"The groups."

When he offers to walk her the rest of the way to her car, she says no, that her car is parked a few paces away.

"I'll come see you." she says, and walks away.

After the dark swallows her, he can still hear the crunch of her shoes on the wet gravel rise above the sound of the rain.

59

He contemplates Blancarosa's arrival as he leans against the patio's brick wall and watches Carmina, with her straw hat and rubber boots on, rake the wet leaves into mounds.

The stormy winds sweep multitudes of clouds along. "If more rain falls over these leaves," he says, "they'll scatter again."

"No more rain'll fall today. Besides, those almond trees have no leaves left."

The clouds move across the puddles. "Why don't you leave with us?" he asks.

Carmina stops raking, looks at him for a moment as though she is considering the proposal, but then continues.

"I'm serious, Carmina. I can talk to Silvia. I'm sure there's enough room for one more—"

"The passion to leave hasn't blinded me," she says. "I'm too old for adventures. Can't you understand? I belong here. This is my place. I'm free here in my own way. We shouldn't discuss this out here. You know what they say about brick walls."

"This'll never change," he says.

"When do you leave?"

"Sunday."

She motions him to follow her to the other side of the house where he can tell her the details about the operation. "I wish you luck."

A flock of birds flies overhead, like scattered petals taken by the wind.

"Will it rain?" he asks.

"All you have to do's let Ochun take care of you in her waters. Let her guide you," she says, and rakes away around the corner.

60

The hours pass and Blancarosa doesn't show. He figures she is kept busy by her work. Perhaps there is someone else in her life. Maybe, he thinks, she isn't meant to be with him. Carmina knocks before she peeks inside her son's room and says Ofelia has come to see him.

"Tell her I'll be right out."

When he walks out to the living room, Ofelia is chatting with Carmina. "Someone must have gone to bed late last night," Ofelia says.

"I read until late."

Carmina excuses herself and goes to the kitchen.

"Want to go for a walk?" Ofelia says. "Summer should come after this storm."

"What's the occasion?"

"My mother said you could come play dominoes with us later."

"Not in the mood to play games."

Ofelia's head tilts downward as though she is looking at the floor or at the mud on her shoes.

"Maybe later. I don't know."

"It helps kill time."

"It requires concentration."

"Only if you play to win," she says. "If you play to have fun—" She draws closer, but stops when Julian leans against the window and looks through the curtain at the street. "You don't have to come. Be honest. Don't trouble yourself with excuses."

"What excuses?"

"I better go." She walks to the door and opens it.

They step onto the porch and stand next to each other.

"I know that lately you've been upset with me," he says.

"I wouldn't be here if I were," she says.

"Look, I don't want to give you the wrong impression. I don't have to tell you the pressure I've been under lately. Time's running out, and I'm scared."

"Don't you think I don't feel the same way. I don't even want to think about what might happen if—" She stops and looks away.

"If we get caught we get caught, but I'm determined to get the hell out."

"Where did you meet what's-her-name, umm, Blancarosa?"

"She was in my history class at the university."

"Did you ever go out with her?"

"I wanted to, but never did."

"I don't trust her," Ofelia says, "but I trust my mother."

"How long has your mother known her?"

"More than a year now. It started when they met at the organizer's house in Miramar. He's the one with the connections in the Venezuelan embassy."

"You've never seen him?"

"Not once," she says, then moistens her lips. Her tan has begun to fade.

"Your mother must know what she's doing."

"And so does Blancarosa," she says, and walks down the porch steps.

"Ofelia," he says, and waits for her to turn to him. "I'll go over later if I can."

She leaves. Moments later, after he watches Ofelia cross the street and go inside her house, there is a knock on the door. He sees the black car parked on the other side of the house. When he opens the door. he finds Blancarosa plucking a coffee bean from one of Carmina's plants.

"Who grows them?" she asks.

"Carmina. Come in."

"Let's go to the beach. It's a beautiful day for it."

"The beach?"

"I want to be close to the water."

Outside, the heat of the day has taken its toll on everything: No longer are there puddles of water on the pavement, or the grass wet, or mud. Carmina comes to the door and introduces herself to Blancarosa. He tells Carmina she is in with the group and Blancarosa gets a serious look on her face.

"We're going to take a drive," he tells Carmina.

"It was a pleasure to meet you," Blancarosa says, then when they walk out: "You didn't have to tell her about me and the operation."

"I trust her like my own mother."

Her car is a beat-up, rust-eaten, 1958 Chevrolet. "Get in, door's open," she says.

"What this car needs is a good set of tires," he says, kicking one of the back tires.

"How bad are they?"

"This one might go any moment."

The top of Blancarosa's bikini shows under her blouse. "It'll take us where we want to go, with a little luck."

The car drives over a pothole and the lid of the glove compartment flaps open. She reaches over as quickly as it opens and claps it shut, but Julian manages to see a radio-transmitter among the grease-stained, wrinkled manuals.

"That's what we're using from the beach to communicate with the boat at Cabo Hicacos."

"You're running a risk keeping it in here."

"I can't keep it at home. The person in charge of *El Comité* lives in the building."

"If you like I can—"

She tells him to look at the construction work they pass on the side of the road.

"Lenin Park's almost done," she says, then falls quiet. Julian begins to tell her what he has been through in the past six months.

61

The sands of Santa Maria beach feel warm in the sun while Julian eats his sandwich and drinks the watermelon shake Blancarosa made. After a while he turns onto his stomach and watches the waves roll, tumble over, and slide far in over the sand. A rich white foam forms over each wave's crest. Blancarosa sits next to him and lights another cigarette. Grains of sand stick in clusters to the underside of her dark thighs and sprinkle off at her slightest movement.

"Isn't this pretty?" she says. The wind tosses her hair back.

He looks at her as he picks up a handful of sand, then watches it fall through his fingers.

"It's us, you know," Blancarosa says.

"What do you mean?"

"Have you ever thought why you want to leave?"

"Because I couldn't make it here."

"That's what you've grown to believe, Julian. Sometimes I ask myself the same question."

"And?"

"I'm leaving because I can't fight the system alone. You and me are the last. See, it isn't our fault. Blame the corruption on the rich people who ran away. The filthy rich. Mill owners. They had the means of changing the way things are."

"You sound like Olivo."

"In a way he's right. Think about it—"

"I have more than I care to," he says.

"What if that first person would've stayed? Fought for what was his." She inhales smoke one last time, tosses the cigarette, and stands up. Once again he is able to admire the dark regions of skin under her bikini as she walks toward the water. Her heels toss up sand. "Jump in," she says, standing against the horizon.

"I'm not wearing shorts."

She laughs, runs to the water, and dives under a wave. Light sparkles on the surface.

No one walks by on the boardwalk.

She returns dripping pearls of water and shakes her hair over him. "Nice and warm, isn't it?" she says.

Julian tries to grab her feet to knock her down on the sand, but she skips away from his reach. "Let me dry your back?" he asks.

"Only if you catch me."

"I'm too tired to chase after you," he says, but he's ready to run after her when he sees the helicopters.

Three squadrons of them appear over the horizon, then Blancarosa stops moving, puts her hand over her eyes, and tells Julian that it is time to leave.

"I want to see what they do."

A strong breeze brings the faint sound of their engines. The sound grows louder as the helicopters draw near.

"What are they doing?"

"I don't know. Maneuvers," he says.

"Let's get out of here."

"I want to see."

"Let's go, Julian."

The helicopters part the surface of the water as they approach.

Blancarosa struggles to put her shorts back on, but Julian tells her to forget them. There is no time. The helicopters are almost upon them. They start away. A crowd gathers all along the boardwalk. Some of the helicopters dive and fire smoke bombs onto the sand. The canisters explode and release red and green smoke. Julian feels confused. He tries to remember where she has parked the car. Paratroopers jump. The sky fills with parachutes.

The rat-tat-tat of the machine guns startles Blancarosa, who searches desperately for the car key on her key ring, finds it, and opens the door. As she drives away from the parking lot Julian looks back to see the parachutes landing in the center of a cloud of red smoke that sweeps into magnificent swirls.

62

"My God. What was that all about?" he asks.

"We got caught in the middle of a demonstration."

"What kind of demonstration's that?"

"Another Bay of Pigs victory celebration."

"They almost blew us right off the sand," he says.

"I'm sorry, Julian."

"How were you to know?"

"You want to go home?"

"Couldn't we go someplace else?"

She asks him if he would like to go to her apartment. "I live alone," she says, "since my parents passed away."

63

She parks the Chevy in front of a paint-chipped, brick building with small square windows. Julian follows Blancarosa into the shade of the stairway. It smells musty there. She climbs slowly, carefully, as though not to make any noise on the stairs' loose boards and give their entrance away. The air, so enclosed, with no way out, smells of soggy limestone.

"Where's *El Comité?*" he asks while she inserts the key into the lock.

The moment she walks in, she tells him not to speak too loud, that the bitch lives right below her apartment.

Tasseled curtains cover the length of the windows, suffocating the room with the day's heat and humidity. She removes her shoes and tells Julian to make himself at home. It is now under the brilliance of the naked bulb that he notices the redness of her face: "Don't worry about her," she adds.

She walks around the glass-top coffee table in the center of the living room. "Relax, I'll be right back."

Three glass panels divide the living room from the dining room. They give the living room an aura of spacious luxury. From an angle a seascape painting— gulls flying low over the water—catches Julian's attention. He has never seen a seascape with such bright colors done with thick brush strokes.

"Did you paint these?" he asks.

No answer.

He looks for the signature around the bottom edge, but doesn't find one.

A cat runs out of a room and jumps on top of the sofa's armrest.

"Ruby!" Blancarosa says. "Don't mind her."

Ruby licks her paws and then yawns. Julian reaches over to pet her, but she paws his hand away.

"Get out of here!" Blancarosa says, chasing the cat out of the room.

"She wants to play."

Blancarosa is wearing a cotton robe when she enters the living room carrying a bottle and two glasses. Her nipples push against the robe.

"Have you ever had any of this?" she says, showing him the bottle of wine.

He tells her never wine, but plenty of *aguardiente.* "Everybody drank a lot of it in the service," he says.

She pours the red liquid into a glass and gives it to him. "Take small sips, you'll enjoy it more that way."

"Did you paint that?"

"No, my brother did. He would have become a fine artist." She looks at the paintings as though she is seeing them for the first time. "Do you like them?"

"Very much," he says, and sips his wine.

"Don't you feel a cooling sensation in your throat?"

He doesn't feel anything, but agrees, thinking that maybe wine takes getting used to. What Fermin would have done for a bottle of this wine, he thinks. The more he drinks, the hotter it gets inside the room. He asks her if he could open the windows, but she says she doesn't like to because the people in the building across the street are snoops, always trying to look and see what she is doing.

A light-headedness dulls his thoughts and slows his reactions. "You know what would be nice right now?" he says.

She doesn't guess.

"Go swimming."

"You can take a shower here," she says, then refills his glass.

"Oh, I couldn't do that. Might leave a mess. I have sand all over."

"Forget the sand. Take a shower. you'll feel better."

"Show me where it is," he says, drinking the rest of his glass. He stands clumsily, looks at his feet as though he might lose his balance. "Hey," he says, "I like the effect."

She leads him through a long corridor where more paintings hang to the end, where she pushes him into the sharp brightness of the bathroom. It is even hotter here. "Promise you'll show me all the paintings?" he says.

"Promise," she says. She pushes the shower curtain aside and opens the faucets.

While she is still bent over he wraps his arms around her waist, turns her toward him, and pushes his lips on her face.

"You're drunk," she says, but doesn't resist him as he thinks she might, but kisses him back. He takes her hands and makes her unbutton his shirt. He pulls her robe down over her shoulders and breasts, moves her under the shower, and feels her breasts swell against his chest. He jumps as the cold water splashes against his back when she pushes him under the shower.

64

"You shouldn't have gotten involved with me, Julian," Blancarosa says, facing the wall.

He feels her spine against his, then, rolling over, says, "Don't say that."

There is a long pause during which he caresses her firm thighs, is lost in the pleasure of her soft skin.

"I shouldn't have let you get involved with me."

"You didn't have anything to do with it. I had always wanted this to happen."

"I don't know, Julian. I fear getting caught."

"So do I, but we can't give up. We have to go through with it."

"Why don't you try again at the Ministry of the Interior?"

"It's hopeless."

Ruby bites the tip of the bedsheet and pulls it away.

"Could you be happy?" Blancarosa says. Her arms look a little sunburned.

"I'm happy now," he says, and kisses her neck and her shoulder. "You make things pleasant."

"Hold me," she says, pushing her back into him.

Julian puts his arm over her stomach until she falls asleep. Ruby climbs on top of the mattress and sits between them, her fur rubbing against Julian's skin.

65

"Nicanor and an officer came by looking for you," Carmina tells Julian the moment he walks inside the house.

"What did they want?"

"They . . . He wouldn't tell me. He said that it is important that he speak to you. He asked me where you were, but I told him that I didn't know. You don't think they suspect—"

"How could they?"

"They'd know, Julian. They'd know."

A look of worry remains on her face as she returns to her cooking. From the kitchen, she mentions something about eating his cod croquettes before the blackout. What Nicanor might want intrigues Julian. Whatever it is, he'd have to confront it. After Sunday he'll be safe. In Andres's room it occurs to Julian that lately Carmina has been staying out of his way, as if she feels that being in contact with him might incriminate her. If he leaves Sunday, the G-Dos authorities will give her a difficult time.

66

He hears footsteps approach the front door, two men's voices, and then someone knocks. He stumbles out of bed and rushes to answer.

"We've found you," Nicanor says.

"What do you want?"

"We come to ask you to do voluntary night-watch duty, *compañero,*" the officer says.

"When?"

"This weekend," Nicanor says. "We need a lot of help with San Lazaro's procession. Will you do it?"

"Could it be some other day," Julian says. "You see I start at the brewery on Monday and I don't want to be late."

"You won't be late," Nicanor adds.

"We need you out there to make sure everything goes all right," the officer says.

He remembers that at this time every year thousands of devotees walk from Habana to El Rincón de San Lazaro on the hills of Rio Cristal.

"The watch'll last until midnight," Nicanor says.

"I'll do it," Julian says.

"Come by and report to me."

Julian knows that by then he and Blancarosa will be on their way to Cabo Hicacos.

Nicanor and the officer start up the street. Julian hears their laughter as he closes the door.

67

Silvia assures Julian Nicanor doesn't suspect anything.

"Where's Ofelia?" he asks.

"Don't tell her I told you, but I think she's upset about something."

"Something."

"Blancarosa and you."

"Is she in her room?"

"I believe so."

"Can I talk to her?"

"Go ahead," Silvia says, then, knocking on Ofelia's room door: "Ofe, Julian's here. He wants to see you."

Silvia opens the door, sticks her head inside, then tells Julian to walk in.

Ofelia is seated on top of her pillow with a blanket wrapped around her thighs. Her hair is combed back and tied in a bun. She is reading a *Bohemia*. Ho Chi Minh is on the cover.

"What do you want?" she says, not looking up from the page.

"I wanted to see you and talk before Sunday night." She puts the opened magazine face down on her lap.

"What have you been doing?" he asks.

"Not much. I've been here mostly. How about you?"

He tells her what Nicanor wants him to do.

"You're going to do it?"

"Not a chance."

"I hope not."

"Why are you angry?"

"Who's angry? I'm not angry." She smiles.

He approaches the bed and sits down next to her. "I think you are. At me."

"Why shouldn't I be? I invited you over because I wanted to be with you, you know, and what do you tell me? That you can't because you don't like games. Then three minutes later you go out with her."

"I admit it was a terrible thing to do, but I had been waiting for her all day. When you came over, I thought you were her."

"I'm sorry I wasn't."

"Look, why don't we become friends first. Maybe later, with time, we—"

"I don't want you as a friend, Julian."

"Why not?" he asks. Then, after a long pause: "You don't know me well enough to have me be your lover."

Ofelia's expression turns sad. Julian can't help but like Ofelia's innocence. Malice hasn't spoiled her.

They fall silent momentarily.

"Have it your way," she says as he stands up to leave. "But, as people say, you don't know what you have until . . . Ah, forget it. Go ahead, leave."

He leaves her room, finds his way out, and decides to go for a walk. Leaving Fermin's house behind in the shadows, he walks toward the spot where he once cut grass for the rabbits.

More than ever, he feels determined to leave. The farther he travels, the more he imagines the things he'll do as soon as he sets foot on the shores of the United States.

68

One hour after Silvia and Ofelia leave for the beach to meet the boat, Blancarosa still hasn't arrived. He thinks about all the things that could have gone wrong. Already he has changed clothes twice, from his best to his most comfortable.

Carmina hugs him as though she were hugging Andres. "Take care," she says. "I'd tell you to write, but I know how you are."

"I'll write you. Send you a thousand letters."

Though she has a cigar in her mouth, she is still able to smile, shows her yellowed bottom teeth.

"You can still change your mind, you know," he says.

She looks at him in a strange way, still perhaps not taking him seriously.

The sound of a car comes from the corner.

"Is it her?" he asks.

"A jeep," Carmina says. "Relax, Julian, you are making me nervous."

"I can't relax." He extends his arms: His hands are shaking.

"Want coffee?"

"It'll only make things worse."

"She'll come."

His throat feels so dry he has difficulty swallowing.

He walks to the kitchen and drinks a glass of water—anything to let the time pass, he thinks. A car door slams shut outside.

"She's here, Julian. It's her. Hurry!" Carmina says, opening the front door and letting Blancarosa come inside. Blancarosa's face looks pale, gives Julian the impression that a terrible tragedy has left him stranded. Grease covers parts of her hands and forearms.

"What happened?" he says, removing pieces of dried leaves from her hair. "For a moment I thought—"

"We must hurry . . . Julian," she says, and takes a breath. "Remember that back tire? The one you pointed out. Well, it blew on the way here."

"What now?"

"I bought a replacement for one hundred pesos."

"Get going," Carmina says. "You've fallen behind schedule."

Carmina walks up to him and embraces him one last time, the last. "May all the gods lead you."

"Next time you hear from me I'll be in Miami," he says.

Blancarosa sneaks behind Julian out through the patio. As he climbs inside the car he sees one of his next-door neighbor's children peering out the window.

69

San Lazaro's procession is in progress by the time they reach downtown Habana. Traffic is dense; the dark streets create confusion. The people dressed in white glitter the way ghosts do: men, women, and children on their knees or on crutches or in wheelchairs, all gathered to honor their promises to the saint.

The crowd delays the car at an intersection. A traffic patrol officer walks up to the window and asks Blancarosa her destination. "We're interned students returning to the university," she says.

"The university is that way, not this way," the officer says.

"There is a detour back there, you know," Blancarosa tells him.

The officer, whose face is protected behind the plastic mask of his riot-control helmet, looks inside.

"I've never seen so many people," Julian says.

"Is this your car?" the officer asks, putting his hand on the leather holster.

Blancarosa hesitates. Her eyes get intense, a cold look about them. She opens the door and steps out. The officer takes a pencil and a pad of paper out of his shirt pocket, moves to the rear of the car, and writes down the plate number. Blancarosa tells Julian to stay inside, then joins the officer.

Julian watches her approach the back. She talks to the officer. He sees her lips move, but he can't read what she's telling the officer.

When she returns, he asks her about what the officer told her.

"We'll be okay," she says. "He's going to check the plate. I told him my father was a volunteer doctor at the hospital."

The officer, after he calls in and talks into his radio, signals the groups of people to stop, clears the path, then waves to Blancarosa to proceed. It works, whatever she told him worked. She drives away as fast as possible. "They can have the car," she says with a nervous smile on her lips, then reaches for Julian's hand.

70

Julian observes how the clouds gather on the sky most of the way. No moon, no stars, only inky darkness. Blancarosa seems pensive behind the wheel, withdrawn from conversation. Insects dart into the headlights down the dirt road. A clicking sound comes from underneath the hood, the engine. When they arrive she drives the car away from the road onto a clearing overlooking the ocean.

"Varadero," she says, and parks the car on the grassy slant of the clearing.

"I can't see the other cars," he says.

"They are there somewhere. No one is supposed to park in the same place."

Tall coconut palms sway behind the foliage. Julian steps out of the car and leaves the door open, as closing it might create noise.

"Watch your step," she says.

"Which way?" he whispers.

She tells him to go ahead of her down the slope, through the mangroves, until he reaches the beach. That she'll catch up to him.

"I have to change into a pair of slacks," she says.

Moist air blows into his face as he walks away from the car. Only the crash of the waves disturbs the peace and tranquillity. Not far from where the car is parked, he waits for Blancarosa.

His heart is racing, the beats pounding between his ears.

"Why did you stop?" she asks after she catches up to him.

"I'm lost."

"We'll find everyone up ahead. Come."

He walks next to her over the white sand, which creeps inside his shoes. He stops, removes his shoes, and it is while he is getting the sand out that he spots a flicker of light from among a circle of dark palms. "There they are," he says.

The closer they draw, the clearer the silhouettes become. Blancarosa finds Silvia and Ofelia sitting by themselves on the scaly trunk of a fallen palm. "Any signals?" she asks Silvia.

"Not yet."

"Three short flashes, one long."

Ofelia turns her wrist to look at her watch. "It's late," she says. "It'll come."

The group grows tighter as the time passes. Blancarosa, Silvia, and Ofelia whisper while he stands against a palm tree and looks out for the boat that is supposed to signal from behind the rocky point of Cabo Hicacos.

71

By 3:45, when the boat fails to show, Blancarosa abandons the group. Julian doesn't see her go, but Silvia tells him she seems upset. When she returns, he tries to calm her. Someone offers her a cigarette.

"I can't think with all of you crowding around me," she says.

"Will we have to go back?" someone in the group asks.

"We have no other choice," another responds.

"It'd be the safest thing," a woman says, "go back and pretend—"

"Christ, what will I tell Nicanor?" Julian says.

"Tell him you went to Habana to visit a relative and decided to sleep over because of the procession," Blancarosa says. "Just invent some excuse."

Silvia tells everyone to go back to their cars and return to the city. "The operation," she says. "is postponed until further notice."

Blancarosa tells Julian to drive back with Silvia and Ofelia so that he won't delay her.

The group disperses and disappears behind the shrubbery. Julian follows Silvia and Ofelia to their car. From the edge of the cliff, where the hidden car looks like a tortoiseshell, he turns one last time to look at the empty waters.

The Shore

72

Daybreak uncovers new possibilities. As Julian walks out of the house on his way to the brewery, Nicanor whistles from up the street.

"I thought you understood," he says, walking quickly. "Shit, I had to substitute for you."

Julian tells him the story he has prepared, that he had gone to Habana to visit a friend early in the afternoon and that by the time he decided to return, San Lazaro's procession was in progress. Nicanor looks into Julian's eyes.

"I'm not playing games with you, Campos," he says.

"Neither am I," Julian says.

"Tell you what you'll do. Return my favor by doing watch duty for the remaining nights this week."

Son of a bitch, Julian thinks, but decides not to argue, for he expected worse.

"I'll be keeping my eyes on you," Nicanor says, turns around, and heads back up the street.

Fermin's kitchen light comes on behind the curtain, and Julian, as he walks by on his way to the brewery, wonders what Silvia will find out went wrong with the operation.

73

After he reports to Polar Brewery's personnel office, Julian is taken to the production line, where endless rows of bottles are filled, capped, and cased. The man in charge of the floor instructs him to check for dirty or broken bottles. Julian sits on a hard wood stool facing a lit panel, in front of which bottles move single file on a conveyor belt. The luminescent panel and the riveting sound of the machinery turning gives him a headache after hours of constant checking for inadequate bottles. Behind the panel, he can see other men sitting, backs bent, picking up bottles, doing the same thing he's doing, only quicker, with more confidence, it seems. After many hours of hearing nothing but glass knocking glass, after rejecting five defective bottles, he thinks of nothing but how in God's name he'll leave.

74

Jasmine fragrance fills the night during the blackout. Returning home, Julian can smell it from a block away. In the house, he eats dinner quickly, washes his face over a pail of water Carmina saved for him, then walks out to begin his watch rounds. Nicanor has told him to go by all the houses in the block and to report to him anyone who looks suspicious.

Instead of wasting his time, Julian walks back to the corner, sits against the telephone pole, and watches the fireflies among the tall grass and shrubs around the trash dump. Fermin's house appears empty, abandoned in the dark.

He grows restless, stands, and goes to the other side of Fermin's house, taps on Ofelia's window, and after she opens it, climbs in.

"You scared me," she says.

"I'm playing watchdog tonight," he says, and smiles, "and burglar."

"Burglar, eh?"

"I have to find out what your mother has learned," he says.

She asks what kind of trouble he got into with Nicanor and whether he suspects anything.

"The lie worked."

"The boat was delayed in Caracas," she says.

"Why?"

"Mother didn't say."

"Did they postpone?"

"You can ask Mother the details tomorrow."

"Don't you know?"

"Not interested."

"Why? Don't you want to leave?" he asks, getting impatient with her.

Ofelia turns her back to him, then breaks the silence by asking, "What's going on between you and her?"

"Blancarosa?"

"Who else?"

"Nothing."

"I thought you two would be lovers by now," Ofelia says. "She looks like the kind of girl who doesn't waste any time."

"I'm not her lover."

"But you like her."

"What's wrong with that? I like you, too."

"You do? But not as much. What do you like about her?"

He doesn't answer, but draws closer to her.

"Have you slept with her?"

"I don't think it matters."

"More than you think," Ofelia says. "Would you be able to tell the difference about which one of us cares more about you if—" She stops talking, then she slowly unbuttons her pajama top. "I have these." She runs her hand between her breasts. "Like she does."

She pushes him down on the bed, then sits on his stomach and pulls his shirt out of his pants.

He feels her teeth sink into his bottom lip; her tongue slips inside his mouth.

"I want you to love me. I've always thought about you and me . . . Prove she means nothing to you."

He cups her breasts and draws his lips to her nipples, bites them gently. She pushes his head down past her navel.

A noise from outside startles Julian.

Ofelia sits still; her face turns to the window.

"I better go," he says. "I'm supposed to be doing night-watch duty. What if Nicanor—"

"You're imagining things. Stay." She runs her hand over his ribs down to his zipper.

Her breasts shake as her hand moves. He leans on his elbows and watches her undress. Naked, she crawls next to him. He feels her warm, smooth skin rub against his.

The excitement grows in his stomach as if at any moment they'll get caught, but he surrenders to the joy of the danger. The more he touches Ofelia, the guiltier he feels, for he knows Fermin would have wanted him to take care of his wife and daughter. She mounts him slowly, eases him inside. The throbbing of his heart feels as if he is running and he can't stop to catch his breath. In her, he rolls over and gets on top.

75

"Stay with me," Ofelia says. "Don't go back to her." She kisses him.

"It's morning. How long have I been asleep?" he asks, sits up, then stands to put his clothes on.

"We fell asleep together."

"I'm late for work."

"I lied to you last night," she says, reaching over to her night table to turn the clock to him. "Mother told me when the boat's coming."

He continues to put his clothes on as though he doesn't care.

"Friday. It'll be here Friday."

"Same place?"

"Further south. Will you ride with us?"

"I don't know. Can we talk about it later?" he says.

She kneels on the mattress in front of him, covering herself with the sheet. "I know I got you."

"Lower your voice."

"Mother's not here. She went to inform Blancarosa last night."

"She hasn't come back?"

"They're probably busy running around."

She pulls him down and kisses him. He starts to climb out of the window when she tells him that he shouldn't forget the fact that he came inside her last night.

76

For the remaining two days and nights, he eats little, sleeps during his watch, and works hard at the brewery. All this, he thinks, in order to forget the operation, Blancarosa, Ofelia, and her possible pregnancy. The only thing he doesn't need right now is a son. Carmina insists that he relax or he will have a nervous breakdown. If she only knew, he whispers under his breath.

He doesn't see Silvia, Ofelia, or Blancarosa at all for a couple of days. During the blackout Wednesday, he is sitting in the usual spot when he hears someone approach. He stands and waits in the shadows.

"Where are you? Campos?" Nicanor says.

Julian doesn't answer. He waits for Nicanor to come closer, then steps in front of him and says, "Here."

"Everything okay?" Nicanor's voice trembles.

"So far."

Nicanor kneels, then sits, pinches a cigarette out of his shirt pocket, and lights it. The flame from the match quickly casts the white of his teeth and eyes yellow. "You like your job at the brewery?" he asks, exhaling.

"Today I broke my record," he says.

"What record?"

"The number of bottles I pulled from the line. Defective ones. Today I removed one hundred and forty three bottles, one with the legs of a cockroach in it."

"It sounds like you are enjoying it."

"Too bad you're not there to share the fun."

"I've had my share of hard work."

"Running the house isn't easy. Is it?"

"Stop being sarcastic. I've struggled to get to where I am today. It's hard to win the trust of the party."

"I can imagine. Look, I'm really not interested in the process."

"Tell me something, Campos," Nicanor says, and stops for a moment. "Can you see me?"

"Not too well in the dark. No."

"Imagine not being seen at all. How would you feel if you had no place, if everyone spat at your feet and assumed you to be nothing but a shoe shiner?"

Julian remains silent.

"It's been the story of my life."

"I'm not in the mood for a political discussion about upper-class cruelty."

"Relax. I won't turn you in, if that's what you are afraid of. I didn't come out here for that," Nicanor says.

He offers Julian a cigarette, which he refuses.

"How do you pay for your smokes?"

"I get paid," says Nicanor. "Like everybody. Then I pay two and a half pesos like everybody."

Julian sits on his heels and scratches the ground with the tip of his finger.

"Ten years ago I lost my pregnant wife in a fire. Can you guess what position she held then? She cooked and cleaned and kept house for the president of Finese Department Stores.

"I was unemployed like the majority of Negroes . . . She and my child burned to ashes.

"No one has ever given me a satisfactory explanation of what happened. I remember knocking on the door of the mansion and being mistaken for a beggar or stevedore. The maid, a woman my own color, sent me to the back door. 'I'll be glad to give you some leftovers,' she said. After the revolution I had my chances to leave, but I didn't. I didn't because I made a promise to myself after my wife died. I promised I'd work hard so that one day I'd attain a position in which I had power. All I ever asked of the revolution was the chance to get even."

"To make people like my father pay," Julian says, driving his heels hard into the ground.

"Not pay. How do you make someone pay for a human life?"

"Tell me the truth, Nicanor," Julian says. "Did you have anything to do with the *gusano* signs?"

"When you're in my position, you've got nothing and everything to do with everything." He laughs, tosses away his cigarette, and stands.

"My father's arrests?"

"El Comité wasn't established when your father lived here."

Nicanor coughs and spits away from where he stands.

"Are you going to reapply for the exit?"

"Until my old age," Julian says.

"You are determined to leave, aren't you?"

Julian wipes his hands on the seat of his pants. Nicanor leaves in the direction of *El Comité*. If that bastard, Julian thinks, heading in the opposite direction, was in his position, he'd leave. The liar. Bernarda told him Nicanor took part in his father's arrest. But it doesn't matter if Nicanor lies, he knows he hasn't said anything incriminating enough to imperil his freedom. He feels as though he is struggling to balance himself on a tightrope. If he falls, he falls for good. No safety net to catch his fall.

At the corner he hears a car skid and speed off, but he doesn't turn quickly enough to see that it is a black car and that its headlights are off.

77

Both floor managers approach him. Julian follows their movement while they traverse the distance of the loading ramps behind the stacked beer cases, then down the dirty aisle between the conveyor belts.

"You are the one," the skinny man says.

"Follow us," the other man says, his long whiskers growing around the corners of his mouth.

"Follow you where?" Julian says.

"Office, *compañero.*"

Julian follows the men to the office. He wonders what insignificant job they are going to assign him this time.

They enter the office, and one of the men closes the door behind him. "How many bottles, Campos?" the man says.

"Unclean ones?"

"No, how many bottles have you stolen?"

"What is he talking about?" Julian asks the skinny man.

"Inventory shows a shortage of five or six cases this week and someone has accused you of taking them. They've seen you, Campos."

"Fools," Julian says.

"Be straight with us." The other man leans against a paper-cluttered desk.

For a moment the complications invade Julian's sense of security; he knows the implications of these accusations. "I haven't been here long enough. I'm here to do a job, not to steal. I'm not a thief. Tell your snitch he's got the wrong man. Tell him to stick his nose up his ass."

Both men exchange quizzical glances, then the skinny one says, "All right, we'll see. Go back to work. But remember, from now on we'll keep you under surveillance."

"If we catch you taking any bottles out of the warehouse," the other says, "you can rest assured we'll kick your ass to prison."

78

"I'm not feeling well," Carmina says with her eyes closed from her bed. She coughs, then spits phlegm into a tin can she keeps on her night table.

"What's the matter?" he asks. He has never seen her in bed so early after dinner.

"I think it's the grippe."

He approaches her and feels her forehead.

"Stay away from me," she says.

"I gave it to you."

She tells him to leave her alone, that she will be better after she has some rest.

"Don't you want me to make you a remedy?"

"I want to rest."

He leaves her alone and goes out to do his nightwatch duty. He sits outside the fence by her window. He thinks about Blancarosa, and how she hasn't called or come by to visit him.

Tonight is typically hot and humid, full of the usual nocturnal noises. But tonight he doesn't mind the crickets or the lengthy howls from distant backyards. He prefers them to the intense noise at the brewery. He closes his eyes to the recollections of his distant childhood, out of which comes a picture he sees clearer than any other: Bernarda is sitting on her rocking chair next to him, outside in the shade of the balcony. She is telling him how his father was taken to the castle and beaten for resisting signing the bakery over to the government.

For a moment he believes he's walking in the darkness of the castle and stumbles upon the scene of men in olive-green uniforms beating up his father. They run away the moment they hear his footsteps.

Someone walks toward him in the dark. Ofelia appears carrying a tray and a thermos. "Crackers and coffee to keep you company," she says.

He thinks he's never been gladder to hear her voice. Julian thanks her and asks her to stay for a while. If only she tells him the truth about being pregnant, he thinks, knowing he won't ask about it. She sits next to him and watches him eat.

"Have one," he tells her.

"I'm not hungry."

"Carmina's not well," he says.

"Mother also."

"A cold?"

"She's nervous. She gets strong cramps when she menstruates."

"I feel guilty about leaving Carmina."

"But she doesn't want to leave, she told you so herself."

"But she's sick."

They share a moment of silence, then Julian speaks.

"Have you thought about what your mother and you are going to do once you get to Florida?"

"Mother plans to start a business, a flower shop. I don't know. I guess I'll go to school and learn the language. And you? What do your parents plan for you?"

"My parents, I doubt they know I'm coming."

"Haven't you written them?"

"I don't write to them. My grandmother did, and I would read their letters, but—"

"Why not?"

"I've never forgiven them for leaving me here," he says.

"Will you stay with them?"

He doesn't answer her question, but instead says, "Too bad there's no guava paste or cream cheese to put on these crackers. Imagine no more scarcity."

"Father always told me about the abundance of everything over there. Did he ever tell you he had been there?"

He tells her Fermin hadn't.

"When he was a child. My grandfather was a cigar salesman. Anyway, Mother hated it whenever he started talking about abundance because there was nothing she said we could do about the lack of it, and the fact that Father always ended up talking about the different brands of Irish whiskey."

Julian remembers Fermin while he licks the crumbs off his fingers.

"I better be getting back," she says, and takes the tray from his side. As she kneels she loses her balance and falls on him. She laughs and says. "See, I really don't want to leave you."

He embraces Ofelia, happy to feel the warmth of her body. and pulls her on top of him down on the dirt.

79

Blancarosa drives up and parks by the side of the house. Julian fears the operation has been postponed or canceled. Dressed in a pair of tight, black pants and a matching blouse, she walks around the car, jumps over two puddles on the sidewalk, and approaches the front gate.

"Attending a funeral?" he asks, standing on the porch, then smiles.

"Funny," she says. "Are you ready?"

"More than ever. Let's go inside."

"I have to go, Julian. I came to tell you that you should go with Silvia."

"Come in and have a cup of coffee."

He leads her into the kitchen and pulls out a chair for her. "Everything's all right this time, right?"

She fans her face with her hands. "Where's Carmina?"

"She's ill."

"Does she know you leave tonight?"

"I told her. So what have you been doing?"

"The usual running around."

Her eyes do look tired, but maybe they look so because she isn't wearing any makeup.

"Why don't you want me to drive with you? You're not upset?"

"I just think it might be safer. Last time I thought we were caught for good, remember?"

There is a knock on the door as he lifts the coffeepot from the flame. He asks Blancarosa to answer. When he turns from the sink, he finds Ofelia and Blancarosa standing by the kitchen entrance.

"Hey," he says, sensing the anger in Ofelia's serious eyes. "Want some coffee?"

"I came to pick up my thermos," she says.

He remembers she took it with her last night.

"I left it with you last night, didn't I?"

"You took it," he says, handing Blancarosa the steaming cup. "Careful, it's hot."

"I've changed my mind," Blancarosa says. "I must go right now."

"Finish the coffee."

"He hates to drink alone," Ofelia says, then leaves, slamming the front door shut.

"See you at the beach," Blancarosa says. She lifts her hands as if to salute, turns around, and leaves. Julian pours all the leftover coffee she left into a small glass for Carmina to use later, wipes the smeared lipstick off the cup, then goes to see Carmina, who is sound asleep. Her forehead feels hot, burning.

"Don't go," Carmina says, opening her eyes.

A thick heavy scent of Mentholatum and *Yerba Buena* comes from her bed.

"I have to," Julian says.

"Something tells me this isn't the right time."

"If Nicanor comes to ask—"

"Forget that son of a bitch. I'm not worried about him," she says in a fatigued tone of voice. "Listen to me. It's you I worry about."

"You can still come with us."

Carmina closes her eyes and keeps them that way as she swallows.

"Is there anything you need before I leave?" he says.

"Postpone," she says.

"It's too late."

She doesn't say anything, but opens her eyes and stares at him for a moment.

"You'll hear from me," he says, moving closer to the bed.

"Forgive your parents, Julian."

He takes her hand, squeezes it, and kisses Carmina good-bye. After she embraces him and he walks out of the bedroom, he thinks, This time there will be no returning.

80

Ofelia doesn't speak to him. Silvia is saying something about the air being chilly and bad for her health, then she continues to instruct the people in the group what to do when the launch arrives. Only two groups of six can board and go to the boat at a time. Ofelia, who is sitting next to Julian, remains silent, but when her mother complains about the air for the second time, she asks Julian if he minds going back to the car to get the blanket she has forgotten in the backseat.

"Maybe when Blancarosa arrives," Silvia says, "she'll have more instructions."

Julian runs up the rocky slope to the car, opens the back door, and climbs inside to look for the blanket in the dark. He finds it on the floor.

The noise of an approaching car surprises him. He jumps into the backseat and closes the door. The headlights of the car cast a blinding brightness. He peeks outside and recognizes the Chevy.

Blancarosa parks the car facing the water, kills the motor, and gets out. She stands by the front fender and looks in the direction of the group. She climbs inside again.

Julian walks over to see what is wrong, what is delaying her.

Blancarosa quickly turns to face him. "Why aren't you down there?" she says.

"I came to get this for Silvia," he says, and shows her the blanket.

"Go back down," she says nervously. "Tell Silvia I have to check on the boat's position."

"You didn't run into trouble, did you?" he asks.

"None. Hurry! We are wasting time!"

He almost slips and stumbles over the rocks on the way down. The dark wood where the group waits lies only feet away. He stops and looks up to see Blancarosa standing near the edge. When he reaches the sand, he looks back again, but Blancarosa is no longer there. He stops to wait for her.

Suddenly the area where the group hides lights up. It looks as though lightning has struck a coconut palm and the woods have gone up in flames. But the brilliance comes from reflectors on the road. Five of them. All Julian hears is the sound of his heart beating. He can't swallow.

A launch's motor cranks in the dark once, twice, but it doesn't start.

"Stop and no one'll get hurt!" a voice shouts over a loudspeaker.

The sound of a machine gun bursts in the night.

Julian runs in the opposite direction while one of the reflector beams begins to chase after him over the sand. He doesn't waste time looking over his shoulder to see it coming, for he can see his shadow moving over the sand.

Another machine-gun round goes off, this one echoing loudly off the cliff walls.

Outrunning the reflector beam, he trips over the blanket and falls on his chin. Sand gets in his mouth. He gets up and wills himself to continue.

This far down the beach, the waves make a loud splash as they crash against the rocks.

A brighter light seems to be drawing closer.

Once when he stops to catch his breath and spit out whatever sand is left in his mouth, he hears the launch's engine trying to start. It turns as though it had choked.

A helicopter flies overhead and its reflector blinds him.

"Stop!" a voice shouts.

He runs to the water and dives in time to be missed by machine-gun fire. Submerged, he feels the salt sting his eyes. He swims underwater until he can't hold his breath any longer, until he thinks his lungs will burst.

The helicopter is circling behind him. He's managed to fool them.

On the surface now, he hears the launch's engine start.

"Wait," he shouts at the dark figure on board.

He reaches the launch. The man pulls him in by the collar of his shirt, then he pushes the gear into top speed and the launch quickly hovers over the dark water.

"Stay down," the man says. "We're almost there."

"Where's the boat?" Julian asks, catching his breath.

"Behind the key."

Julian sits up and turns to look back at the beach. Blancarosa, he thinks, snitched on them. That's the reason why she was carrying that transmitter. That's why she stayed back, delaying, radioing in the group's position.

"If we don't move fast," the man says, "the coast guard'll catch up to us."

Now the helicopter turns and heads in their direction.

The man turns the wheel and the launch sways behind the key. They slow down to wait for the helicopter to fly over, then the man takes a flashlight out of his back pocket and signals at the boat three times.

The roar of the helicopter fades, turns, and draws closer.

"Stay down until I tell you," the man says. "We have to make a run for it now. We're doomed if we stay here."

At full speed, the launch bounces over the water, slicing the waves. Then, once it reaches the boat. it pulls sideways and slams against the hull. A rope ladder drops over portside. The man motions for Julian to climb and Julian begins to go up the ladder quickly. As quickly as he can without getting his feet tangled.

"Keep your right hand and your left foot on the rope," the man says, climbing after him. "Then alternate. Watch me."

Julian looks down and observes how the man climbs.

"Hook the launch to the winch!" a voice shouts over portside.

"Forget it, we don't have time," the man says.

Julian reaches the top and two black hands help him over.

The man makes it over, orders the men to get the rifles, then tells the navigator inside the cabin to give it all it's got. He takes Julian to starboard and orders him to sit under a strewn canvas tarp, which covers the line skeins.

"Stay here. I'll come get you as soon as we're safe."

Julian sits under the tarp and tries to catch his breath. He hears the voices and the fast squeaks of footsteps on the deck.

Under the tarp, the smell of fish overwhelms him. He feels the soaked shirt stick to his skin. Salty drops of water trickle from his nose to his chin. In the meantime, he can't stop thinking that at any moment the boat will be stopped by the coast guard. A soldier will come, kick the tarp off him, expose him, put the barrel of his machine gun to his temple, and pull the trigger.

81

All of them betrayed. Silvia and Ofelia are dead. Who knows what'll become of Carmina? He shouldn't have made it, he thinks, but he was lucky. His breathing has now returned to normal, but the humidity under the tarp is unbearable.

Blancarosa betrayed them, but why didn't he see it coming. What a good job she did in fooling everyone, the bitch.

Footsteps pass by outside the tarp, and he can't help but tremble with fear.

If they find him, let them shoot him. He envisions himself being thrown overboard, wounded, blood oozing out of the tiny bullet holes. He'll struggle to stay afloat, and then the scent of his blood will attract sharks, which will circle him until they sense he's weak. They will bite and tear his legs off first, then his arms, while parts of his skin float around him, his blood staining the water a dark crimson.

He thinks the coast guard is waiting for the boat to near free waters before interfering. Something tells him they are waiting. Waiting. They'll come for him and they'll catch him and kill him, then it will all be over.

82

Julian loses all sense of time, of how long he has been hiding under the tarp. He feels the heat of his breath. The sun must be rising, he guesses, while the motor vibrates on the deck boards. Someone lifts the tarp off. "You can come out now," the man who brought him to the boat says.

"Where are we?" Julian asks. The sun is coming out and it blinds him momentarily.

"On our way. We'll dock to refuel in Nassau."

The sun rises over the horizon and creates the most wonderful hues of yellow Julian has ever seen on the water. The man extends his hand and pulls him up. Julian stretches his legs. The man steps inside the cabin, pours coffee into a tin cup, and gives it to him.

"Too bad not everybody—" the man begins to say, but stops. His appearance isn't rough or weather-beaten, but clean shaven. He leaves Julian, who leans for support against the side of the cabin under a porthole and fights seasickness as he slowly sips the bitter coffee.

Gusts of wind make the flags on the wires overhead flap. The ship rises and dips and parts the water into white crests. On the other side of the boat, in the vastness of the ocean, the clouds and what's left of the night seem to vanish like smoke.

83

The winch cranks to a start and the fishing net drops over the stern. Water splashes over the deck, then falls through the scuppers.

He tastes the bitterness on his palate while the net, crowded with fish, is reeled in. The men in knee-high rubber boots ease the net down on the deck. As soon as they open it, the fish spill everywhere, their scales glittering as they snap their tails.

"Are you hungry?" the man says. coming up behind Julian.

Julian notices the man's Venezuelan accent for the first time.

"We'll be in Key West in no time. Relax, man. You are safe now."

"What time will we arrive?"

"You'll know the moment you see the shore. You know what your compatriots call them? The shores of exile."

Julian remains quiet and watches a flock of sea gulls hover over the boat.

"Will anyone be waiting for you?"

"No one," says Julian.

"You'll be all right," the man says and smiles. "You Cubanos seem to do all right everywhere you go."

"Will I have problems with the authorities?"

"Don't worry about authorities. You are a refugee seeking asylum. Let me handle them."

The man smiles then crosses his hands behind his back and walks away whistling some Venezuelan song inside the cabin.

A fish fight breaks out among the laughing men, who, knee-deep in blood and dead fish, throw entrails at each other.

The Refuge

84

Julian recovers at the Catholic Refugee Center. Padre Marcelo Gomez, the parish priest, helps him adjust. The padre finds Julian a temporary job in a small cafe on Calle Ocho in Little Habana. Something, Padre Marcelo had said, to get Julian started in Miami until he locates his parents.

A day after his arrival, after he is questioned for hours and cleared through a security check at the immigration department, Padre Marcelo drives him to the center. Drugged by his own weakness, Julian still thinks of Carmina, by now being harassed for answers, and of Silvia and Ofelia dead. He tries to avoid thinking about the two people killed when Ofelia was shot. His son or daughter, his own flesh and blood. To forget, Julian watches the heavy traffic of the downtown streets. Men in short-sleeved shirts and women and girls in summer dresses fill the sidewalks, browse through sales racks outside shops.

Padre Marcelo gives Julian a list of items, the most frequently used phrases in the English language, so Padre Marcelo assures him. "Hope they keep you from getting lost," the padre says.

Slowly, Julian peels the piece of paper out of an envelope and reads the list:

MY NAME IS JULIAN
I LIVE AT THE CATHOLIC REFUGEE CENTER
GOOD MORNING
HOW ARE YOU?
WHAT IS YOUR NAME?
WHAT IS THE MATTER?
I AM LOST
CAN YOU PLEASE HELP ME?

And so on. Julian doesn't feel up to reading any more. His eyes tire easily. He closes them and tilts his head back against the cushions on the front seat's headrest.

But as the days elapse Julian adapts readily to his new situation, being in a new place. The feelings of strangeness fade. He learns some of the easier phrases on the list. Repeats them constantly, trying to memorize them. The words slip out of his mouth while he keeps his concentration on the way each sounds. He knows that his first and most important move is to learn the language, and he feels confident he can do it.

He learns more words and silly-sounding phrases at Downtown Miami Café, though the customers speak more Spanish than English. His boss, Betancourt, likes him enough to let him eat free meals. Julian has never seen such an abundance of food, meat mostly. Whenever he opens the meat refrigerator and sees the sweet ham, roast beef, bologna, mortadella, and cheeses, his heart throbs, then he can't escape thoughts about Ofelia, especially that night she told him about her father having been here in the United States.

Padre Marcelo visits him often during lunchtime. He says he still is trying to find his parents. Julian's third day at the center is his most difficult. Padre Marcelo gives a requiem in Silvia and Ofelia's names.

During the middle of the Mass, Julian can't stand it anymore and walks through the side door outside. He stands under the archway, not knowing what to do next. The feeling of being lost scares him. An old, thin American woman approaches. She is being led by her white poodle. The dog stops, sniffs, and lifts its hind leg to urinate on every other tree on the way. Julian imagines the dog mistaking the woman's skinny legs for a tree. He laughs. The woman stares at him with a humorless look on her face, then turns her face in the other direction.

After a while Julian goes upstairs to his room, from where, out of the window, he has a view of the street. White buildings, two or three stories high, fill the panorama. White, he thinks, is the color of grandeur.

The following night he has a nightmare in which he hears the sound of the helicopter, then the machine guns. When he wakes up, there is the twap-twap of the helicopter flying overhead. He gets out of bed quickly, afraid, and walks to the window, but doesn't dare to stand in front of it to have a look outside. He knows he's afraid. and at the same time he tells himself he's not a coward. What could happen to me here? he thinks. He waits, then the helicopter comes into view. It circles the block with the beam of its reflector light spilling over the rooftops.

In the morning, Doña Isela, the woman in charge of the kitchen in the center, comes and wakes him up. She tells him someone got shot on the street last night.

"How's your English coming?" she asks.

"Good morning," Julian says, trying his heavily accented English on her.

She smiles and tells him he already sounds like a native.

"Will you be returning from work early?" she asks.

"I don't know."

"Padre Marcelo wants to have dinner with you."

After he changes into the clothes Padre Marcelo bought him in the clothing store at the corner, he comes down the stairs and walks outside, where immediately the heat reminds him of Habana after it has rained and the smells of wet asphalt and earth fill the atmosphere.

Sometimes, when he is not concentrating, he thinks he is back, on his way to the university, to the Ministry of the Interior. He shakes the vision out of his mind, assuring himself there is no Malecón at the end of the street, no university, no Capitolio, only, here in Miami, white buildings. Houses and hotels in which the people sit and relax on lounge chairs on their balconies or in lobbies. There is no reason why he should be paranoid here in Miami. Miami is safe, but then he thinks of what Doña Isela told him about that person getting shot.

Betancourt is scraping the melted cheese with a spatula off the surface of the grill. He is a man in his late forties, heavyset, with the type of kind eyes and crooked smile that give a God-isn't-it-nice-to-be-alive sort of impression.

"What's the matter?" Julian says to him in English.

"Ah, you're coming along," Betancourt says. "I'm glad you are here early. Today's going to be busy. Fridays are always like that. Being payday, everyone comes from the bank across the street."

Julian takes two eggs and cracks them open over the grill.

"Christ, Julian, I just cleaned that," Betancourt says.

Julian tells him he hasn't had breakfast.

"Sooner or later you better start eating at the center," he says. "You are going to eat your way through my profits." Betancourt's face grows stern. "Besides," he adds, "the girls around here aren't attracted to fat men." Betancourt taps his beer belly.

"All this food won't get me fat, it'll take more than this to get me fat. *Los gordos mueren contentos,*" he says. Fat people die happy.

Julian smiles to let Betancourt know his feelings are not hurt. Betancourt walks over and slaps Julian's arm, then says, "Go ahead and eat all you want."

"Padre Marcelo wants to see me this evening. Can I leave early?"

"Good news?"

"I don't know."

"Maybe he's heard from your parents," Betancourt says.

Julian shrugs and backs away from Betancourt, who moves to the cash register.

Julian enjoys working the cash register better than the grill, though he still feels uncomfortable counting the correct change when customers pay their bills. The heaviness of the rolls of coins. The stacked bills in the tray make him think of how he will try to get ahead in this country, make a new life for himself.

The hours pass rapidly between the groups of customers, and by the end of the afternoon, Julian leaves the café to go see Padre Marcelo.

Walking through the streets of Miami makes Julian uncomfortable, perhaps because he is still not used to the signs and symbols and lacks the necessary sense of direction to get from one place to another. One wrong turn and he will be lost. The good thing about finding his way to the center is that the steeple of the church is tall enough that he can see it from a few blocks away.

Padre Marcelo waits under the archway. The way Padre Marcelo stands, hands behind his back, his short black hair neatly greased and combed over his bald spot, and the way the loose skin under his chin rests over the tightness of his white collar, bring Julian relief.

"Good afternoon," Julian greets the padre.

Padre Marcelo puts his arms around Julian's shoulders. Julian follows the padre up the stairs, which at the moment are lit in wonderful bright colors as the sun goes down behind the stained-glass windows.

"Isela has made tea, would you like some?"

"I'd much rather have coffee."

"She will make you some," Padre Marcelo says, then laughs.

"What's so funny?"

"Nothing, son. She will make you the coffee, but you will have to listen to her lecture on why coffee is bad for your nerves."

Upstairs, Julian wants to sit down and rest his feet. Why does walking make him so tired, he wonders, when he is so used to walking?

"I have located your parents," Padre Marcelo says, entering the dining room where Doña Isela is getting the table ready for dinner. "They are not in Miami, but in Los Angeles, California. In a place called Bell. I spoke to your mother. She said your father is on his way here. After I spoke to them, he took the next available flight."

While Padre Marcelo speaks Julian tries to remember what his parents look like. He cannot remember much about them. Only that even before his mother had left, her hair had begun to whiten. His father's voice comes to Julian in the screams he so often heard in the night. Then the fire, the slow burning flames.

Padre Marcelo rises from the dinner table, upon which now the silverware shines against the white embroidered tablecloth, and approaches him.

From the kitchen comes Isela's singing while the coffee brews.

"Will you go with your father?" he asks.

Julian shrugs.

"The best thing for you right now is to have someone take care of you, put you through school, get you a better job."

"How can I forgive them?" Julian says.

There is a long pause. Doña Isela brings Julian a cup of coffee and returns to the kitchen to get dinner served.

Padre Marcelo stands next to him, puts his hand on Julian's shoulders once again, and says, "If there is any hatred in your heart, you are in the perfect place to get rid of it."

The sky is dark now. The streetlights have come on. The people still on the streets will eventually find a place to go.

"Your mother asked me to please talk to you, convince you to go with your father. If God had intended for you not to reunite, then he never would have allowed you to make it this far."

Julian moves away from Padre Marcelo and leans against the wall by the window to sip his coffee. It is hot and burns his lips. He watches night fall. The blinking lights of an airplane move across the darkening sky. Now he wonders if his father will be on that flight.